Before her death in July 1997, beloved lesbian-feminist author Chris Anne Wolfe published two Amazon adventure novels – *Shadows of Aggar* and *Fires of Aggar*. But these two volumes are only the first half of the four-part Aggar cycle. Chris Anne also published two stand-alone novels – a time-bending romance, *Annabel and I*, and a retelling of Beauty and the Beast, *Roses and Thorns*.

As her publisher and friend, I was honored to inherit the manuscripts of Chris Anne's remaining novels, short stories, poetry and songs. These hand-written volumes include both remaining Aggar books – *Sands of Aggar* and *Oceans of Aggar* – and more than a dozen retold fairy tales, and original fantasy and contemporary novels. Only Blue Forge Press has the right to publish Chris Anne's work and we take great pride in that mission.

Jennifer DiMarco
Publisher
Blue Forge Press

Annabel and I

by Chris Anne Wolfe

Blue Forge Press
Port Orchard † Washington

Annabel and I
copyright 1990, 2013, 2014
by Chris Anne Wolfe

ISBN 978-1-59092-934-6

First Edition February 1996
Second Edition July 2001
Third Edition March 2004
Fourth Edition September 2007
Fifth Edition January 2014
Sixth Edition January 2023

Cover photo by Jennifer DiMarco
Interior art by Chris Storm

For information about film, reprint or other subsidiary rights, contact: blueforgegroup@gmail.com

This is a work of fiction. Names, characters, locations, and all other story elements are the product of the authors' imaginations and are used fictitiously. Any resemblance to actual persons, living or dead, or other elements in real life, is purely coincidental.

Blue Forge Press is the print division of the volunteer-run, federal 501(c)3 nonprofit company, Blue Forge Group, founded in 1989 and dedicated to bringing light to the shadows and voice to the silence. We strive to empower storytellers across all walks of life with our four divisions: Blue Forge Press, Blue Forge Films, Blue Forge Gaming, and Blue Forge Records. Find out more at www.BlueForgeGroup.org

Blue Forge Press
7419 Ebbert Drive Southeast
Port Orchard, Washington 98367
blueforgepress@gmail.com
360-550-2071 ph.txt

"This book is for all women-loving-women
regardless of role, closet or political correctness.
Because there are as many different ways
to love a woman as there are women who love women;
it's the loving, not the label, that really matters.

"This book is dedicated to Elizabeth.
She asked for a story of cherished care...
for a romance to celebrate magic and joy.
Without her request, I might never
have gotten around to sharing this particular
fantasy with anyone.

So please, snuggle beneath your favorite quilt
with a mug of something hot and a bit of starlight,
and enjoy this gift I wish for you —
this tale of *Annabel and I*."

—Chris Anne Wolfe
1960 – 1997

Annabel and I
by Chris Anne Wolfe

Dear Lucy,

There are people who live extraordinary lives filled with decisions and deeds which seem destined to mold the fiber of history. To keep an accounting of such folk seems right and would be an easily defensible task, I think.

But my life?

I am barely twenty-seven, a writer of children's stories, and the proprietor of a summer fishing lodge. True, I am the only woman proprietor in the area, but it was more a matter of chance and fortune (my uncle's retirement and my mother's money) which brought me to settle on Chautauqua Lake than any conscious plan. There was no struggle — no great obstacle to be overcome in my life's course.

Still, a life may be extraordinary simply in its circumstances.

I can feel my Beloved smile. Annabel has always reminded me how miraculous it is that our lives have ever even touched. It is because I know she is right, and because I want you, young Lucy, to have a truer accounting of your heritage than a forged birth certificate, that I am preparing to write this now. For you see, though Annabel and I are both twenty-seven, I was born in the summer of 1960 — she in the spring of 1879.

I don't know if you will believe our story, Lucy. You are only five now and too young to be told yet. But perhaps when you come of age it will answer the questions of who your real papa was and why your two aunts live as we do — and why your Great-Grandmama will one day sit in the room and wish you well.

It will be your own decision to believe or not. I confess, I don't know what I would think if someone sat me down and spun this yarn for me. After all, we each know only the truth of our own reality. But I know the magic in mine. I know, because my beloved Annabel shares it with me, and there is simply no greater truth for me than the warm clasp of her arms.

So, for you Lucy, and for you my Beloved, here is my accounting of our beginnings.

Jenny-wren
10/12/87

Chapter One

What I remember most about Uncle Jake is his gentleness. It was such an odd contrast to his huge, bulky strength. Even as I grew, his stature never seemed to lessen, although when a man weighs in at over 200 and easily clears six feet he's apt to look a lot like a lumberjack to other adults too. But he wasn't — a lumberjack, I mean. He was a fishing guide and the owner of a summer fishing lodge on Chautauqua Lake. His hands were callused from tying barbed hooks, sanding down wooden hulls, and rejuvenating dilapidated generators. He put salt blocks out for the deer in the winter, took in his half-orphaned niece for the summers, and chopped wood when he got angry about things. In all the summers spent with him, I never once heard Jake raise his voice in irritation.

That was the sole thing he had in common with his brother, my father. I never heard Father rant or rave about anything either, but Uncle Jake kept his voice calm because he believed nothing was ever solved by shouting... crying, maybe; talking, probably — but shouting, never. Father, on the other hand, simply never noticed anything worthwhile enough to get angry about. His life revolved around the chemistry lab at the University. How or why he ever married has always been beyond my comprehension. That his marriage could be deemed successful would require a redefinition of the word, though if asked I'm certain he'd maintain he'd found nothing to complain about. Unless he remembered me, then he'd probably chew on the stem of his pipe and nod a bit before recalling that everything in life has its drawbacks. Needless to say, I never really thought of his house in

Chicago as home.

Neither did Mother, I think. The summer I turned three we began going to Uncle Jake's. He was an "old" bachelor even then and enjoyed having us around as a ready-made sort of family. His sweetie, Mrs. Stevens, was a dear and welcomed me into her domain (the lodge and kitchen) as if I was one of her own daughters. She taught me how to cook, how to laugh — how to like being a woman. It took me years before I understood her husband had run away with someone or other and hence she was neither divorced nor widowed. However, Uncle Jake was a stolid admirer of hers regardless of the disgrace of her status.

Small towns are great for disgrace and gossip, though neither Uncle Jake nor Mrs. Stevens ever bothered to come right out and confirm or deny the rumors of their relationship. She ran the lodge proper while he ran the fishing and boating end of the establishment. She lived downstairs in the back rooms during the summer and spent the winters up the road with her daughter's family. But she never dated another fellow after her man left; she just spent summer evenings on the porch with Jake. And Jake spent every Christmas down the road with her kin.

They were my family. It was none of my business who my uncle slept with. It was a code that was subtly but distinctly drilled into me. Bedroom affairs were private. If you respected someone, you let them be. That was all there was to it.

Sometimes I wonder if that's such a sophisticated attitude or if it's just an excuse for hiding? Probably a bit of both. But I was raised in a small-town place despite my mother's intentions. Maybe if she'd lived, she would have succeeded in instilling me with a little more rebellion against the "bourgeoisie."

Unfortunately, all she actually succeeded in doing was stirring a desperate longing for home. Not for Chicago particularly, but for some place safe and secure. Some place consistent that didn't change floor plans, languages or people quite so much. Some place where I belonged and where I had roots... a place like Uncle Jake's.

It was sheerly convenience that we summered at Chautauqua every year. Uncle Jake's familial fascination with me, his only niece, was merely an added benefit for Mother. It meant she had a perpetual baby-sitter between him and Mrs. Stevens, and it was a thing she took perpetual advantage of.

That's sounding wicked and I don't actually mean it to be. Mother was an artist by trade and by soul, and the summer classes at the Chautauqua Institute were some of the best in the country, if not the world. Sometimes she taught, sometimes she studied, but all the time she left me to my own devices. Although that was only for the summers, the winters were something quite different.

The year I was five she took me with her to London, where I was taught to read rather early by a very competent nanny. At six it was private tutoring in Rome, and I also learned that my mother was near famous for her paintings. At seven it was Paris, and I discovered I had absolutely no sense of color, but I found refuge in Twain, Milne, and Kipling. At eight it was Zurich and Lucerne, where I discarded sketching entirely to replace it with music lessons; I fell in love with the "barbaric" guitar. (Patience had never been Mother's long suit, but to do her credit she did provide a music instructor amidst the odd collections of tutors and sitters she supplied me with.)

Then in August of 1969, just before we left Chicago for Amsterdam, Mother's car disintegrated on the expressway. A semi with a flammable cargo jack-knifed coming down an on-ramp. It was during rush hour; mine was not the only family with tragedy that day.

I was nine.

Father, being his usual implacable self, sent me off to Amsterdam as scheduled. It was the first year I was to be officially enrolled in any school and the place boarded most of its girls, so arrangements were not hard to modify. I think I was in The Netherlands by the end of the week, but I'm not sure. I don't have very clear memories of that time. I only remember pecan-waffle cookies, a small church in an out-of-the-way back court, and Emily Dickinson; it was the year I discovered poetry and loss.

I was growing up rather quickly.

The next eighteen months taught me much. I learned to share feelings with paper-and-pen or music, when there was no one around left to share with. I learned my father was just as content to have me in Chicago, attending the Catholic girls' academy around the corner as in Europe, so I spent only the one year in the Netherlands. And I learned that Uncle Jake would fight to have me in the summers; Father agreed once I simply voiced my preference for the lake and the country. Being a city man who could not visualize life without laboratories, academic libraries, and lawyers automatically attending to bills and patent rights, he could not imagine anyone actually preferring rural living. His younger brother was an anomaly Father rarely spared a thought for; his wife had been involved with Chautauqua, so that had not been undefinable — one occasionally made sacrifices for one's work. But his daughter?

Well, country air was good for growing children. And so I was allowed to continue the tradition established by Mother.

I never asked Father if he was glad to be rid of me for those three months each year. I only knew I was glad to be rid of him.

As I said, those eighteen months taught me much between boarding school, Uncle Jake's and Chicago. I learned the difference between obligations and love — and Uncle Jake loved me. During the school years, first in Amsterdam and later in Chicago, he was always there. Never a letter writer, Uncle Jake faithfully sent me a postcard every week and phoned every month. Diligently he kept track of every question I would write whether it was about snow storms, Mrs. Stevens or missing my mother. Then every second Sunday in the month, when he phoned, he'd answer those questions.

When I was older, Mrs. Stevens confided in me that he'd kept half the county supplied with firewood the winter I was in Amsterdam. He and my father had never been able to talk things out.

Little wonder that the summers I had once longed for became the summers I literally lived for. Summers and Uncle Jake meant going home. More and more I felt as if Chicago was merely a boarding house from which I attended school, and breathlessly I'd await the summer holidays and home. Those feelings only grew as the years wore on... as I came to know myself and Annabel better.

It was late August in the summer of '71. I had just turned eleven. The sky was a very clear blue with barely a cloud in sight. An unusual occurrence to say the least, because Chautauqua County in New York usually got more rainfall than Portland, Oregon. But it was such a beautiful day that it will always stick in my memory. Hot but not blistering as the breeze was cool enough, and around the lake the hills huddled, green with maples and pastures. It was the kind of day I loved perhaps, simply because they did come so seldom.

Uncle Jake sat grinning and rubbing his reddish beard, shaking his head at the tiny croppie I'd just fished out of the lake. The boat swayed a bit as he chuckled and grabbed my line, gently taking the little acrobat in hand to unhook it.

"Jenny-wren, I don't know how you do it." His dark eyes sparkled at our familiar jest. "You always find the smallest critter about."
Brown eyes which matched his, a crinkled-up, freckled nose, and ruddy red pigtails all stared back at him with my widest grin.

"What're you planning, ehh?" He tossed the silvery bit into the water. "I know! You're teaching them to bite and get let off, so you can catch'm easier when they're proper big keepers!"

"Maybe so," I stated, sticking my straight, little nose high into the air. But I couldn't hold the pose and dissolved into laughter with him.

The breeze tugged on the fishing line, and I lowered my rod tip as he got a better hold of the swinging hook. He reached overboard, barely rocking the huge, old rowboat, and hauled the minnow bucket up over the side.

A squeal of protest and laughter rode out on the light wind then. And alerted to the sounds of peers, I squinted towards the shoreline.

"We're almost out of bait, Wren. What do you say we—" his voice trailed off as he followed my gaze.

A figure in white pants and sweater sat laughing on a giant, worn rock as a smaller companion — obviously a girl — stood calf deep in the water holding her skirts high as she reached for a drifting sailboat. The model was caught in the stubborn breeze, and even the gentle lapping of the waves towards the shore couldn't quite reverse its direction.

"I bet I could get it for her," I spoke, half-requesting the opportunity.

I felt Uncle Jake's grin more than saw it, because my eyes were glued to those little square, white sails.

"Haven't been so many girls about to play with this summer, have there?"

At that, I did look at him. Then with something of a blush, I shrugged. "Hasn't been so bad."

"Wanna bet?"

I shrugged again. Pre-adolescents are not always the most communicative even with adults they love and trust.

"So, how far you think it is?"

With a blink I turned back to gauge the distance. "Only a couple hundred yards or so."

"Or so—" he added meaningfully, but this time his grin was a reassurance. "Well, I guess you managed the cross-lake swim easy 'nough last week. This ought to be a cinch."

"Ought to," I agreed cheerfully and reeled up my line, quickly hooking the barb to the rod.

"Leave your T-shirt on," he advised sternly as I slipped out of my canvas shoes and shorts. "Bathing suit's not enough in this sun. Your nose is already going to be burned to a crisp."

"Is not. I put lotion on like you said." But I didn't take my top off. I really did have an awful lot of freckles already.

"And mind your toes."

At that one I stopped in mid-scramble and peered overboard questioningly. "Why?"

"See their dock?" He pointed at the well worn, wooden length. "It's long because there's a shelf along the lake shore here."

"Then why doesn't she just wade out and get her boat?"

"She's right where she belongs, if she doesn't swim."

That was an astonishing thought to me. How could anyone be spending the summer at the lakeside if they didn't swim? What kind of girl was this anyway?

"We could just row over and get it," Uncle Jake suggested, noticing my stillness.

"Not on your life!" and I hopped over the side as he started to chuckle.

"I'll be watching," he called then. "No fancy stuff—"

Fancy I didn't need, but after years of globe trotting, I knew the value of a good opening when I saw one. It had never been particularly hard for me to find playmates, yet I knew how much easier it was to be included in a game if I was returning a stray ball or offering to add a doll to the tea party, then if I was just a bystander trying to get in. It was something my nanny in London had taught me very early on.

It wasn't a very long swim at all, and I paused a few yards from the small boat, pushing the wet bangs out of my eyes. Then with my best overhand crawl, I came up to the thing.

"Hey?! Hey you! That's not yours!" The white clad jester on the rock resolved itself into an adolescent male. "Just what do you think you're doing!?"

I stood up. The boat hadn't even cleared the edge of the shelf yet.

"I said what are you doing?!"

He was an obnoxious looking boy with dark hair falling into his eyes. He raked his fingers through it, only making it worse. And his scowl wasn't in the least way cordial.

"Don't you want it back?" I shouted with my most practical, grown-up manner. "It's not going to do you much good out in the middle of the lake, you know."

"Why you little—"

"Yes please! I would like it back."

I grinned at her. She was my age but not as stick skinny as I. Standing there with her navy blue skirts clenched up about her knees, showing her white bloomers — bloomers? Geez! Was there a grandmother in charge of dressing her? But she was smiling and looked much friendlier than that older one; I barely resisted making a face at him. Politeness can be prudent, though. So I knelt back down into the water and cautiously swam their model in.

I was proud of myself; I made shore without scraping a knee or water logging their toy. And as I stood up to gingerly walk in the last few, stony feet, I must have been beaming.

"Bother, it's another bratty girl—"

My chin jutted out and my eyes burned a hole through his measly, scrawny body.

"Oh don't mind Dickie. He's fifteen and on his

way off to England for school next month."

"Yes, don't mind me at all," he reiterated distinctly, picking up a discarded book. "I've decidedly more important matters to attend than playing beach guard for a pair of silly—"

"A lousy guard too," I interjected rudely. "Can't even save a stupid boat."

He turned kind of red and stomped off... which suited me just fine. I hate insufferable people; male or female, they are the worst commodity civilized humanity has yet to create.

A delighted giggle brought me back, and I grinned as she confided, "I've been wanting to do something like that for days—" She turned and walked out of the water still talking, "He's been with my great-aunt's people for most of the summer. And honestly, I wish he had stayed. I don't give a fig for any old school in England, and he parades about here as if he's some long lost Duke of Windsor!"

"Is he your cousin?"

"Regretfully, no." Her hair was tied in a blue ribbon matching her skirt and sailor-styled blouse. And as she turned, she pushed the ends of a ponytail over her shoulder. "He's my brother. Four years older and a hundred years ruder."

Her hair wasn't really so light brown, I noticed. It was shining with all the bronze and gold of autumn if you looked very closely.

"I hope he didn't hurt your feelings—?"

Startled, I realized I was staring and abruptly thrust the ship at her. "Here. It's all right, I think."

Her eyes were the color of liquid cinnamon. They made me smile as we stood there toe-to-toe.

"I'm Annabel," and impulsively she put out her hand.

"Jenny. Jennifer Cassel from... from the lodge across — other side of the lake there." She had a great handshake. Not at all flimsy, and I grinned even broader.

"Standishes from Philadelphia," she supplied, both hands firmly about the model boat again. "I'm — we're here with Grandmama for the summer."

Curious, I eyed the sweeping, green lawn behind her. Most of the property was hidden from the lake by the line of elms, willows, and maples. But beyond, a yellow, Victorian house with white gingerbread trim sat cheerfully back on its small crest.

"Nice," I admitted. "I'm just around for the summers too. I come live with my Uncle Jake. He runs the fishing lodge over there. In the winter, I go to school in Chicago in the winter — live with my father."

Her eyes shadowed with sympathy, "Your mother is gone? Both of my parents are too. They died when I was still young."

"Well...," I shrugged awkwardly, "Mother's been gone two summers now."

Her hand touched my arm. She understood. It wasn't the grief so much as the awkwardness at being different.

"Oh—?" she glanced past me, startled.

I turned, looking back over my shoulder towards the lake.

"Is that your uncle?"

"Yep." He was rowing in with his usual unhurried, powerful strokes. Behind Annabel I noticed someone coming down the lawn. "Is that your grandmother?"

Annabel spun about briefly, "Yes." Her grin was infectious as she faced me again. "I suppose they're about to inquire of each other's business and decide if we're suitable acquaintances or not."

"Should we be friends anyway?"

She looked at me seriously for the longest moment. Then with a decisive little nod, agreed. "I think we shall." She offered her hand again to seal it.

"And who do we have here, my child?"

"Grandmama, this is Jennifer Cassel." Annabel lifted the model for emphasis. "She swam in and rescued my boat for me."

The solemn countenance of the silver-haired matriarch disappeared with her smile, and the kindest, grey eyes I'd ever seen turned to me. "I'm delighted to meet you, Miss Jennifer Cassel."

I felt like I should courtesy or something as I recognized the eloquent lilt of the Oxford-tinted English which was learned in European boarding schools as a second language — impeccably learned and from a very exclusive school, Mother would have interjected. I kind of nodded and stuttered, "Ma'am."

"Please, Grandmama Standish. All of Annabel's and Richard's young friends call me such."

"Thank you—" and I actually felt like smiling again.

"No, it is we who thank you. It seems you appeared exactly at the moment Annabel most needed you today."

"Oh... well, I didn't really do anything special or—"

"Nonsense, child." But the way Grandmama's gentle voice enfolded me was warm like a hug. There was no rebuke in her words. "Each of us can be special — or magical, if we want to be. And you are no exception.

"Now," she nodded towards the dock as I heard Uncle Jake's familiar step clump down the planks,

"Who do we have here?"

"It's her uncle. Her father's brother—?" Annabel glanced at me tentatively.

"Uhm — yeah, my Uncle Jake. I mean, Joseph Cassel."

"Good afternoon, Ma'am," Jake pulled the floppy, old, fishing hat from his head. He wiped his lake-watered and fish-smelly hand down the side of his overalls before offering a handshake.

I missed what they were saying as a small piece of me died in mortification. There Grandmama Standish was, some grand descendant of nobility, clad in high-necked, black lace from head-to-toe talking to my seemingly hick-town uncle who looked nothing like the prosperous, well-educated son of the deceased industrialist. But I did myself credit. I straightened my backbone, reminded myself of all those shallow people I'd met between Amsterdam and Chicago, and I stubbornly refused to be swallowed up by the earth. He was my uncle and the best there was anywhere.

The strain of pretending no disgrace and the internal shame of needing to pretend at all had its price, however. I remember absolutely nothing about the rest of our visit. I know we stayed for lemonade. But it was Uncle Jake who determined that though the Standishes were returning to Philadelphia come end of the week, they would be spending the next summer here once more at their lake house. It was he and Grandmama Standish who arranged for Annabel and I to see each other the weekend after the fourth of July.

To this day, I thank the stars that Uncle Jake was there after all. Left to my own devices, I never would have managed to see Annabel again!

The Second Summer
Chapter Two

D ickie says — one oughtn't climb trees, if one is to be a lady."

I looked at Annabel curiously, hanging upside-down from my tree limb in order to face her. The lacy trim to her dress was torn, her sash was askew, and the inevitable white bloomers were dusted with tree bark and grit. As she sat there, swinging a leg, unperturbed and munching on an apple, Annabel didn't seem to care in the least for what Dickie had said.

"Grandmama doesn't quite agree with him, you know. She always—" Annabel paused to unravel her hair ribbon from an inquisitive twig, then continued with, "She says — a lady is best suited to do whatever a lady best wishes to be doing."

Pulling myself upright, I puzzled that one out. I seemed to be missing an important concept somewhere. "What's Grandmama call a lady?"

"Any grown-up girl, silly."

"Oh."

Her cinnamon-brown eyes surveyed me thoughtfully. We made quite a contrast with her in lace and ribbon and me in jeans and pigtails.

"What do you call a lady then?" We were slowly learning that words often seemed to mean different things to our different families.

I shrugged. "When my father says act like a lady, he means I should mind my manners. But Uncle Jake only says to learn what it is I want to do and just keep on doing it. He says thank you very much, but he doesn't want any feather-headed lady for a niece. He says he likes me the way I am."

"Hmmm... " The apple was forgotten for a brief moment. Then with a crunch, she bit into the fruit and mumbled, "I don't think Grandmama thinks ladies are necessarily empty-headed."

"Definitely not!" I clamored down and closer to her, settling on a limb just other side of the tree trunk. She handed over the apple, and I managed a too-big-bite before returning, "I mean, Grandmama couldn't think they're all empty-headed. She's a lady herself, isn't she? And she's not like that."

Annabel giggled, "Not even Dickie could argue around that one."

"So she must mean *woman*." I had her full attention again, and I hugged the tree trunk as I leaned forward eagerly. "Uncle Jake says 'woman' instead of lady. And a woman has the right to be whatever she is, simply because she is."

"Like Grandmama's lady? A lady can do whatever she pleases and still be a lady, because she just is?"

"Exactly. I mean, what else could she be? It's not like it turns her into a monkey or something. If you climb a tree it doesn't make you anything."

"True. It's being a lady and doing a thing that makes the thing lady-like."

"Or so your Grandmama would say," I grinned, honorably crediting the one deserving of it.

"And—" Annabel added significantly, "as your Uncle Jake would agree."

"I think," I decided, tossing aside the apple core and swinging myself down into my usual hanging position again, "that I agree with them myself."

"Why?"

"Because I don't like empty-headed girls, so why

would I like empty-headed, grown-up girls? At school, all they worry about is sneaking off and trying on new eye make-up or telling stories about their sisters' boyfriends. It only gets them into trouble with the nuns. I mean, school is for learning. Why go if you're only interested in your sister's love life? Stay home with the soap operas, for cryin' out loud."

"Soap operas?"

"Boring romance stories. Some crisis or other is always happening—"

"Then, why don't they?"

"Oh, they have to go — at least 'til they're older. Maybe there's hope for them yet."

"Well, I like school." Annabel leaned over the top of a tree limb on her stomach, her feet dangling. "Or rather, I like my tutors. Grandmama has all sorts of interesting acquaintances in Philadelphia, and they're often recommending someone or other as a teacher. And I like learning... except for Greek — and Latin. Dickie says, the stories are too hard for girls to understand, but I think it's the old languages they're written in. When Mr. Beaumont translates the chapters for me, they're not at all difficult to follow."

"You study Latin?" I came upright, my mouth open in astonishment.

"I hate Latin. I hate Greek. I hate everything but English. I can't ever make the sounds right and those stupid old verbs just don't make much sense."

"Does Grandmama make you study all that?"

"No, I suppose not." With a sigh, Annabel plopped down to sit on a lower limb. "But that's part of the problem, you see. The stories are so interesting — all about those old gods and goddesses, and I want to read them. I truly do! But the only books in English are so dull. They're positively tiresome. Poor translations, Mr. Beaumont explained. So if I want to read about Hera outwitting the great Zeus or about Ulysses' perilous adventures, then I have to master the old tongues first."

"That's not right," I frowned, trying to remember the thousands of titles on the bookshelves at Uncle Jake's and in my father's library.

"What's not right?"

"I know it isn't." I concentrated harder, my most perturbed scowl surfacing.

A gentle hand reached out and touched my forehead, startling me from my thoughts.

"Your face will freeze that way someday, Wren, if you frown so ferociously." And her voice was as soft as her fingertips had been.

"But it's not right."

"Frowning will make it different?"

Different translations, that was it!

"Different versions!"

"What are you talking about?" and it was Annabel's turn to look perplexed.

"There are different translations and different versions. All the stuff for kids is watered down."

"Watered down?" With a patient sort of sigh, Annabel reminded me of my peculiar expressions. "Wren, I don't come from Chicago."

"Yes, but — I mean, there are translations for children and then there are translations for adults. I know Ulysses' travels are translated in full — by scholars with awards and everything, because my father has this copy on his bookshelf at home. A colleague of his at the University received special honors for revising the translations, while keeping the adventuresome overtones of the originals."

"And it's in English?"

"Has to be. The only Latin or Greek my father has time for these days is in a chemistry equation."

"Do you think—? Oh, I suppose it's a very special edition."

"It was published for lots of universities to use. I shouldn't think it'd be too hard to find." I grinned with sudden inspiration. "The bookstore at Chautauqua Institute might have it. They have nearly everything else."

"They would—?" Annabel looked dubious. "Grandmama wants very little to do with their self-righteous thinking."

"Then I'll get it for you. One of Mrs. Stevens' grandchildren works there this summer. She could find out!"

"Do you think so?" Her face lit up with anticipation, and a touch of mischief worked its way in with, "Should I dare?"

"Absolutely. Grandmama wouldn't care. Not really. She's always saying, we should read more books and try new things. Isn't she?"

"Oh, it's not her I worry about. As long as Grandmama doesn't have to deal with the preachers and prudes herself, getting the books from Chautauqua would be fine by her. But if Mr. Beaumont hasn't spoken of these translations, then?"

"Then *he's* the one being provincial and small-minded," I announced with authority. "Besides, are you a lady of Grandmama's or of Dickie's?"

She laughed, her bloomers showing again as she slipped upside down herself. "Do you need to ask?

"Oh no!" Annabel abruptly pulled herself back up onto the tree limb. "M'dam Randolph's here with her people!"

"Who?" I bent a bit sideways to get a better look

at the lakeside through our leafy camouflage. All I could make out was a brightly painted row boat pulling in to dock.

"They're friends of Grandmama's. M'dam Randolph always comes in by the lake, like you and your uncle do," Annabel explained hurriedly as we scrambled downward. "It means we're late!"

"Ut-oh! Mrs. Hodges!" I gulped and jumped the last half dozen feet to the ground. "We were supposed to help with the tea cakes today!"

We tore up the hill for the pantry doors to the kitchen. Mrs. Hodges was a forgiving, mothering sort of woman and she'd be apt to have us do the washing up later rather than subject us to lecturing reprimands — if Grandmama didn't catch us first. But the trees hide most of the lake shore from the house as well as much of the hill's wide lawn and gardens from the beach. So, Grandmama's guests caught no glimpse of our mad rush for the kitchen's sanctuary... and we were simply lucky, because apparently neither did Grandmama from her parlor windows.

The Third Summer
Chapter Three

Uncle Jake and I walked around the dangling shrouds of the willow trees which hid the main house from the shore. He grunted a bit in approval at the sight of the well-tended grounds and gardens. "Take a good look at those elms there, Jenny-wren. We aren't going to be seein' them ever look so healthy again with this blight sweeping through."

"What—? Oh, yeah. Sure." My stomach did a nervous flip-flop. But right now I didn't care a hoot about Dutch Elm Disease and stupid trees! All I cared about was Annabel! Then the world suddenly leapt to right itself as I saw her waving from behind the verandah railing.

"See! There she is, Uncle Jake! I told you they were expecting me."

His bear-sized hand squeezed my shoulder gently, but his steady stride continued forward.

"It's all right. Really it is—"

"I believe you, Wren. But sometimes things come up and plans need to be changed."

I stopped in my tracks, feeling like my precious one-day-a-week visit was even closer to evaporating then it had been before.

"Come on now, Honey." He paused, watching me patiently. "No sense in anticipating the worse. Let's just put it down to neighborliness, shall we? After all, I haven't had the chance to stop and say a proper hello to Mrs. Standish yet this summer."

My feet moved like disgruntled tree roots. But I followed anyway.

Annabel's enthusiastic wave caught my

attention again, and I squinted a little. Uncle Jake was right, something was wrong. She had always been down at the dock to meet me on Thursdays. But today she was just sitting there.

We climbed the steps as Uncle Jake's deep voice rumbled, "Well, well — lookey here."

"What happened to you?!" I cried, dropping my wind breaker on the railing as I hurried near.

The old, wicker wheelchair creaked as Annabel shifted, making a comical grimace. "Dickie was right. Ladies shouldn't climb trees."

Her right leg was plastered protectively and extended straight, looking very uncomfortable. I hugged her awkwardly, afraid of hurting her.

"Good morning, Mr. Cassel." Grandmama appeared in the open doorway as their local girl, Sally, swept through with a tray of iced glasses and lemonade. "Would you stay for a glass of something?"

"Be my pleasure, Mrs. Standish." Jake waved towards the table, his hat in hand.

"Hello, Mr. Jake—"

"Good morning there, Missie. Did I hear you say something about a tree?"

"Yes, sir," she mumbled, subdued again.

"You'll have to excuse my granddaughter," Grandmama smiled indulgently as Sally left us. "She's gotten a bit stale with all of this inactivity. I'm afraid she's never been forced quiet for any period much longer than a day."

"No need to apologize," Jake chuckled, gazing fondly at my friend. "I've been set-up a couple of times in my life with a broken bone or two. I remember the feeling well."

"Does it hurt awful?" I asked urgently.

"No," Annabel looked disgusted at herself. "It

aches a little from being up so much. That's all."

"When did it happen?" Jake asked, settling his frame cautiously into a cane chair.

Grandmama's grey eyes twinkled as she prompted her grandchild with a lift of an eyebrow.

"Friday... sir." Annabel gathered herself together a bit, straightening in her chair. "I was climbing our tree and fell. Dr. Morely said my knee was badly sprained and my fibula appeared to have a slight fracture." She looked at me then, adding, "The knee hurt more than the other, actually."

"Just climbing, eh?" Uncle Jake eyed me suspiciously. He'd seen me scamper through enough trees to know my antics; there wasn't a doubt in his mind what I'd been teaching her.

I squirmed and got absorbed in my lemonade until he took pity and turned back to Grandmama. "How long do you expect her to be laid up, Mrs. Standish?"

"Another five weeks, I'm afraid. Dr. Morely believes she is young enough that it will heal quite as it should. But he would prefer to take a cautious route. Especially," she shared a smile with Uncle Jake, "since there are such a great many trees about."

He chuckled.

"Five weeks?!" I felt alarm stirring again. "That's the rest of the summer!"

She looked miserable, "Yes."

Uncle Jake got his worried sort of look, his thumb stroking the side of his beard. My stomach twisted as he cleared his throat. It was never something I wanted to hear when he did that.

"Perhaps it would be better, if I didn't leave this young hooligan with you today, Mrs. Standish. It appears, you've got quite a handful without Wren here."

Annabel stopped breathing, sending her grandmother a silent, panicked plea.

"Not such a handful," Grandmama assured him with her quiet, implacable calm. "Sally is here in the mornings, and naturally, my housekeeper, Mrs. Hodges, is always about.

"Actually, Mr. Cassel, my problems lie less in the direction of competent help and more to my granddaughter's amusement. I'm afraid there is only so much an elderly grandmother and a middle-aged housekeeper can do to occupy a thirteen-year-old invalid. I was wondering if there might be some sort of arrangement we could make that would allow young Jennifer to visit more frequently?"

Uncle Jake lifted a bushy brow at us youngsters but graciously counted Grandmama with, "I would disagree with you describing yourself as 'elderly,' Mrs. Standish. Age, if I may say so, lends only harmony to enhance your grace, Madam."

Grandmama nodded slightly, flattered; but she wasn't about to give Jake time to find any objections. "I do realize it might logistically be an inconvenience for you to have your niece visiting us very often, and I am somewhat at a loss to help since we have no transportation to speak of. But I do assure you that Jennifer is quite welcomed and that I have never found her to be any more mischievous than my own here—"

His eyebrows shot up at that and my throat went dry.

"Please, Mr. Jake?" Annabel beseeched with such a tremulous hope that I found myself clenching my fists in helplessness. "It would mean so much to me. And I do promise, I'd be especially good. Grandmama wouldn't have any added trouble."

With a gentle hand he leaned over to cover my curled fists, and our eyes met. His softest voice wrapped around me as he nodded, "Means that much to you, Jenny-wren?"

"Sh-she's my best friend, Uncle Jake."

"And best friends do for each other," he smiled. Slowly he opened my hands, rubbing the nail bruises on my palms. "All right then. If you can keep up with your chores, I don't see why not."

I squeezed his hands tight and found tears to blink back. "I'll get the chores done."

"All rightie," he sat back again. Grandmama smiled approvingly. He drew a breath, putting on his business-like frown and stared at me again. "When and how?"

Annabel bit her lower lip and glanced back-and-forth between us.

I swallowed nervously. "After guitar lessons, maybe?"

He chuckled and at Grandmama's inquiring expression elaborated, "She has her father's gift for simplifying things."

That was news to me.

"Sounds good, Wren," Jake grinned openly. "Have to send a boat up to Chautauqua to fetch you anyway, they might as well drop you here. Then come sunset, I can swing by on my own way in with the fishing tour and get you." He nodded again to his hostess, "Good thing you just live across the way and not all the way down in the lower lake. But—" he sobered at a thought, "It is going to leave you a long day, Mrs. Standish. Her lessons get done 'round noon on Mondays, Wednesdays, and Fridays. I wouldn't get here until eight — eight-thirty usually. You sure you want her all three days?"

"I think it will do quite splendidly," Grandmama returned, rising.

"If she gets to be a problem, you let me know." The steely note in his voice was meant for me.

"If she gets to be a problem, Mr. Cassel, I will simply put her to work in the garden."

His chuckle grew, sprouting into deep laughter. Grandmama could handle me just fine.

* * *

It was the best of summers. We lamented over the romance, tragedy and poetry of the Brownings. We rallied around the hand-copied speeches of Margaret Fuller and Susan B. Anthony — which Grandmama produced from somewhere or other to distract us on one particularly sultry afternoon. But it was our desecration of Shakespeare with our pre-adolescent exuberance that kept Mrs. Hodges laughing in stitches and Grandmama hiding chuckles behind lace kerchiefs.

I learned, too, about vegetable gardening as I tried to keep up Annabel's small plot for her. On sunny afternoons, she'd sit in the shade reading aloud as I weeded through the dirt in my tattered jeans. She laughed only once when I pulled up a small tomato plant. I'd thought it was a weed. But she never teased me about it.

Together we discovered the wicker wheelchair wasn't any good on beach rock, but it was manageable on the back lawn. My muscles toughened, and Mrs. Hodges taught me how to lift properly so that I wouldn't hurt my back helping Annabel about. We spent hours brushing out my ruddy colored hair, trying French braids and interesting knots — or massaging her good leg to keep it from growing too numb as she sat so still.

Then too, Grandmama hired a local artist to come and give Annabel lessons in watercolors. It had been something Dickie suggested in a letter from England. He had claimed 'all the girls of best breeding' dabbled in music or painting or something. That had not been a recommendation of much weight with either of us.

"But Grandmama, I don't want to be an empty-headed, soap opera girl like Dickie thinks I need to be!"

Grandmama Standish lifted a brow slightly at the odd reference to operas, and she looked at me briefly, fully knowing I had a tendency to introduce Annabel to strange terms such as this one. But Grandmama was not one to be distracted from any topic. "There is no need for you to worry about becoming an empty-headed anything, Annabel. As much as it might please your brother to see you embrace conventions, this is not the point under discussion."

"Yes, Grandmama," Annabel returned in more subdued tones. When Grandmama took on this no-nonsense attitude, both Annabel and I knew there wasn't any use to more protests.

"You quite enjoyed your sketching instructions over this past winter, Dear. Is there some reason you should find art any less enjoyable here than you did in Philadelphia?"

"Well, I suppose there isn't." The idea did begin to take on some appeal, once removed from Dickie's arena of influence.

"I also seem to remember, Mr. Edward Bannister paid you quite a compliment on the composition in one or two of your pieces when he and Christiana were visiting."

"He did say something of the kind, didn't he?"

I glanced at Annabel, acutely aware of the excitement suddenly sprouting.

"Very well then, I'll make the arrangements, and you'll begin next week." Quite satisfied, Grandmama smiled at us both. Then she slipped away, conspicuously leaving the half-filled lemonade pitcher on the porch table — along with a full bowl of sugar cubes.

"Hurry! Sally or Mrs. Hodges may be coming to clean up soon," Annabel whispered urgently from her wheelchair. "But careful!"

In one nervous convulsion, I caught my breath and saved the slippery glass pitcher from shattering. Then with the utmost caution, I started to pour again.

"Leave enough room to stir the sugar—"

For my own glass, the warning was a little late. But I nodded and did better with hers. I set the pitcher down, heaving a mental sigh. Sometimes, I really did feel like an awkward klutz. "So? Who's Mr. Bannister? Your art teacher back home?"

"Oh no, he's one of Grandmama's artist friends. He and his wife live in Rhode Island — started the Providence Art Club there." She drew a long, cool drought from her lemonade and breathed a very satisfied little "hmm."

"Did you like him?"

"Well yes... he was kind enough. I only met him this past year. I don't think Grandmama's known him as long as some of the other artists and writers who keep visiting us. But she's known his wife, Christiana Cartreaux, from before the War. They'd see each other whenever Grandmama went with Grandfather to visit the Boston offices."

"Is he a good artist? And did he really think you were good too?!"

"And Mr. Bannister really thought you were good?"

"No, he's not simply good," Annabel corrected me quite matter-of-factly. "Mr. Bannister is a very good artist — his landscape won the Philadelphia Centennial Exhibition, you know. But he did say, he liked some of the composition in a few of my sketches."

"Oh."

"I have an awfully long way to go, Wren, before anyone like Mr. Bannister might say I was good at drawing or painting. An awfully long way, indeed."

But that summer, she did make a good start at it.

What I remember most clearly about that August, however, had nothing to do with her painting or my music. It had to do with our friendship.

It was a dampish Monday, with a steady drizzle. The lake was a steely sort of grey with splattering, little holes from the rain. Damp and misty even by mid-day, the chill wrapped around me as I stepped off the boat, waving Stan — Uncle Jake's youngest guide — off to the lodge. Then for the longest of moments, I simply stood there, the rain trailing down my old, green poncho. The sound of the motorboat receded to nothingness before the mist had even enveloped its shadowy figure. Somewhere a lake loon trilled. Smiling, I returned the warbling whistle — the only birdcall I knew. The silence stretched, then it answered me, and I felt a warmth rise inside.

The trees rustled with their dripping leaves, and my footsteps echoed on the dock with a dullness that carried only a scant few feet. The boathouse looked cheerful and bright, the mistiness hiding its peeling paint and dirty windows.

I felt contentment spark within myself and begin to burn like a steady flame. This was my lake. Rain or chill made no difference — and I felt a million miles away from Chicago.

My tennis shoes were soggy and squished as I trudged up the lawn. The tomato plants and zucchini vines looked thoroughly drenched, but happy. A bit like me, I thought, moving on towards the house. The lace curtains in the parlor fluttered, and I raised a hand in greeting, hurrying as I climbed the porch steps.

"Mind the carpet!" Annabel cried as I burst in, the wind rattling the door as it shut.

Startled, I looked at her a bit oddly. But I carefully stepped to the side, back onto the floorboards.

"Ohh — you're going to have the entire place soaking. Mrs. Hodges!" and her little, brass bell went peeling.

"Heavens," the stoutly housekeeper tisk-tisked in through the dining room. "You'll catch your death of cold, Miss Jenny."

"She certainly will—" Annabel seconded, wheeling her chair nearer only to have the parlor's door sill catch her wheels and force a halt.

"Sorry—" I gingerly handed over my dripping garment.

"And your shoes. Mrs. Hodges, don't we have a spar pair of house slippers about? She can't wander 'round this drafty, old place without something decent on her feet."

"Quite so." The housekeeper cheerfully confiscated my muddy footwear too. She seemed completely oblivious to her young mistress' exasperation. "I'll see what I can find for you, Miss."

"And tea!"

Mrs. Hodges paused, turning back to nod politely. Then she scuttled my disgraceful things off to the service porch.

"You're awfully late," Annabel announced, going to turn her chair about. But the door sill was still being difficult. "Oh crimanie! I wish they'd just throw this whole, silly contraption into the rubbish! Well — aren't you going to help me?!"

I jumped, pulling my hands from my pockets again and attacked the chair back.

"Careful!"

I almost unseated her. I suddenly didn't seem able to get anything right.

"By the fire."

The carpet tugged. The oriental rug's fringe caught in the front wheel bearing, and I ran over the edge of her lap shawl, pulling it to the floor.

"Why do you even bother?" she challenged angrily, and I stepped back, abandoning all attempts to help.

Worriedly, I shoved my hands into my back pockets and danced from one foot to another.

"Miss Jenny—!"

I looked gratefully towards the hall at Mrs. Hodges' voice.

"Would you come see if these slippers will do?"

I glanced at my friend's frowning face.

"Go!" she snapped.

I bolted, running from my own confusion.

The kitchen was warm and bright with the wood stove's chrome gleaming, the smell of fresh bread baking, and the plaster walls of whitewash keeping the gloomy day well at bay. Mrs. Hodges turned from the pump at the sink and with a smile nodded to the old satin house shoes beneath the butcher block table.

"Thank you," I muttered, finding them big, but cozy enough.

"Miss Annabel is lashing your ears red, tisn't she?"

I blinked, startled, and met her kindly gaze.

"It's not you, Miss Jenny." She chuckled and put a plate of scones beside the tea cups on the tray. "It's the rainy day here. She's been short-tempered and holier-than-thou all morning."

"She has?" I echoed weakly.

"Herself retired for a nap, you know. She said the child would tire herself out by dinnertime and not to expect Herself down before then."

"That bad?" I began to think that maybe it hadn't been completely my fault, when the lap shawl had caught and the rug fringe had snagged.

"That bad," Mrs. Hodges tisked, reading my relief for what it was. "We all have our bad days now'n'then, Miss Jenny. Especially when we've been tied to a chair with an injury. Bear with her, and she'll right herself in good time."

I pursed my lips at that, then scowled, remembering how good it had felt to be standing out in the rain at the end of the dock. It didn't seem fair to lose that just because she was feeling irate!

"Now then, Miss, the tea's there ready. Will you take it in for me?"

"Oh — yeah, sure."

Annabel glanced up at my appearance. A small frown tugged down the corners of her mouth, and then her attention returned to her book.

Resisting the urge to sigh, I carefully set the

tray down on the coffee table. The delicate curves to the thing's legs always suggested that it was about to collapse, but then I'm not a lover of French ornate inlays or ornate anything, so my mistrust was understandable. The cups clattered as I turned them over, preparing to pour, and she threw me another dark scowl that I managed to ignore.

With a measured breath, I paused, the silver teapot in hand.

Of all the rooms here, this was my very favorite. The odds'n'ends of attics and old houses filled it. The carpet was a deep shag of amber and the oriental area rug was rich in blacks and reds although its edges were too frayed for repair. Heavy velvet drapes of faded peach stood guard beside the lace curtained windows, and the Chippendale armchairs and sofa were covered with intricately embroidered florals. And there was a fireplace, its depths filled with a nice blaze today that popped cheerfully, and the mantel reminded me of a home I'd never really had, all cluttered with brown-tinged photos and knickknacks.

The room smelled of lemon oil and burning pine. All'n'all I thought it was a nice, old room to spend a rainy day in.

"Is there any honey?" a disgruntled voice muttered.

Well, a nice place if the company improved. I filled the china cups.

"I asked, if there was any honey?"

"I heard you," I returned calmly, adding a teaspoon of sugar to my tea. "But you didn't ask very nicely."

"My... aren't we Miss Perfect today!"

"Miss Perfect wouldn't have nearly dumped you out of that chair nor pulled the shawl off your lap." I sat back, snuggling into the old satin pillows, and curled my feet up under me. "Neither would Miss Perfect have arrived like a drenched cat. Now, are you going to stop being a bitch or should I just go help Mrs. Hodges in the kitchen for the day?"

She stared at me in utter shock, her eyes wide and her mouth half open.

I put on my most blasé twelve-year-old Chicagoan attitude and stuck to my guns. With the kind of deliberate calm I could remember my mother using, I merely sat and sipped my tea.

"What did you call me—?"

"A bitch." I couldn't tell whether she was horrified or disbelieving, but I still wasn't backing down. So I forced a shrug and expounded, "You're sure acting like one."

"I am not!"

"You are too!" and my saucer went down with a clang.

"All I did was ask if there was any honey!"

"All you did was ask for honey?! For honey, for dry carpets, for perfect wheelchairs, for extra slippers, for help with the chair but *not* with the shawl — for tea in the middle of it all! And you don't even take honey!!"

"Oohhh! Then take the tea away! You're being perfectly horrid!!"

"No, *you're* being perfectly horrid. I bounded up the steps to come in here happy an' — and glad to see you. Then find you all ornery and snapping at me before I can even get out of my coat! So it's you who's being perfectly horrid — to me!" I flounced up and out of the room with the tea tray in tow.

"Come back here!"

I hit the kitchen door with my behind and swung through.

"Well my goodness!" Mrs. Hodges looked me up and down, my cheeks bright red and my mouth set so stern.

The little brass bell rang, frustration jarringly evident in its not so cheerful timbre.

Mrs. Hodges wiped her hands on her apron front and eyed me suspiciously as she went.

With a sullen pout of my own, I tabled the tray and took the cups to the sink to rinse. The old, metal pump creaked beneath my rough handling, until begrudgingly, it gave up an icy slosh or two.

The door swung through as Mrs. Hodges returned. "She says she wants you."

I shrugged and washed the cups in the standing basin of soapy water.

The bell peeled again... a long, jangling complaint.

"Well?"

"We're having a fight," I replied succinctly.

"Not a very fair one if you can walk away from it and she can't, I'd say."

I shrugged again, rinsing the cups and saucers for the last time.

The bell stopped.

"She told me to take the tea things away," I maintained quietly and picked up the scones to replace them in the cookie bin. "I told her I was going to help you instead of sitting with her, unless she could act a little nicer."

"And what did she answer?"

"She snapped at me."

The housekeeper tipped her head a bit as if to say 'that was that' and went on about skinning the carrots for the dinner roast.

The bell rang again. A rather short, almost

timid ring this time.

"Jenny—"

I set about washing the scone plate.

"Please?!"

It was faint, but I couldn't ignore it.

Reluctantly I sighed and set the small dish in the sudsy basin. I didn't really like being mad at her. It just made my stomach feel ucky.

Mrs. Hodges tactfully said nothing as I walked through the kitchen door.

I made it as far as the dining room across from the parlor. With a toe scuffing over the rug fringe, I put my hands in my hip pockets and bumped back against the doorjamb.

"Wren—?" she'd moved as far as the parlor entrance, managing not to get the wheel stuck this time. "I'm sorry, Wren. Will you please not go away?"

I scuffed the fringe in the other direction and shrugged. "Mrs. Hodges says you've been like this all day."

There was a painful silence. I glanced up to see her worrying her lower lip and staring at her hands.

I shrugged again, admitting, "I was really looking forward to... to seeing you today — and all."

Her eyes misted. "Were you?"

"Yeah," I managed a nod.

"So was I."

That caught me and I met her gaze.

"I wanted to show you something, but then—"

I shouldered my way out of the dining room. "But then what?"

She took a deep breath, blinked the tears away, and waved at the windows behind her. "Then it started raining and — and I was afraid I wouldn't be able to show you. And then I was afraid you wouldn't even be able to come."

That helpless feeling was back as I mumbled, "I can't change the weather."

"I know." Her voice wobbled a little. "I'm sorry. It just... it just felt so awful being cooped up in here waiting, not knowing one way or the other."

"You never even said hello," I whispered, poking at the floorboards with my toe again.

She smiled faintly and offered, "Hello."

I looked up again, then straightened and repeated with a little more enthusiasm, "Hello."

"Are we still friends?"

"Of course we are!" She took me by surprise with such an outrageous idea, and I planted my feet firmly. "I mean, it's just a little bit of a fight, isn't it? It's not like anybody's trying to kill someone."

Her smile grew with a choked-off laugh, "No one's died that I can see."

Swallowing hard, I remembered my own part and offered, "I'm sorry too."

She looked at me.

"I knew — or at least, Mrs. Hodges told me. This is just kind of a bad day for you, being laid up and indoors. I could have been nicer—"

"You weren't at all really."

"I know. I got angry at you for spoiling our day. I guess," I shrugged, "I shouldn't have called you a bitch. I'm sorry."

"No one's ever called me anything like that before," she murmured.

"I didn't mean it. Least," I amended with an embarrassed grin, "you aren't usually."

"That awful?" But there was mischief in her eyes now.

I nodded. "Mrs. Hodges thinks Grandmama's

getting a nap to get away from you until dinner."

"Oh dear," she giggled.

"I won't do it again."

Her rather practical, considering look descended as she thought us over. Then slowly, her blond-brown hair swirled and she shook her head with a definitive, "No. I think, actually, if you can't call me.... Well, if you can't say such things to me, Wren, then who's going to be left to honestly tell me what a boar I'm being?"

"Best friends do that sort of thing."

"Both ways."

"Then I guess we shouldn't stop."

"Fight or no?"

"Fight or no." And my stomach uncurled. I felt ten feet tall, because she really did want to see me after all.

"Can I show you now?"

"Sure," I grabbed the back of her chair, "where to?"

"The side window there—"

We maneuvered around the end table and didn't even lose the shawl. We got as close to the window seat as we could get her, before she made me climb over her leg and pull the lace back.

"I don't know if he's there today."

"Who's there? Where?"

"Under the woodpile out by the pines there. He'd stolen an apple core from the garbage Saturday morning, and I saw him huddled in, eating it. Yesterday I tossed some nuts out and this morning too. He came yesterday afternoon, but I haven't seen him today!"

"*Seen who?*"

"A   porcupine.   The   dearest,   little   baby

porcupine. He's not much bigger than a ball of yarn, and he's all bristly with the cutest little black nose. Oh, he's got to be out there somewhere."

"I see him! There, at the far end. He's got silverish spikes!"

She craned her neck, stretching to see around the velvet drapes. "Yes! That's him, Wren. That's him. Isn't he adorable?"

"Drenched," I corrected.

"Like someone else I know."

I grinned, abashed. "I like rain."

"So does he."

He certainly looked like he did. Quite unperturbed by the dripping logs about him, he turned a pine cone over in his paws as he munched away at the nuts inside.

"Does he have a name?"

"Not yet," Annabel squeezed my knee excitedly. "I wanted to wait to show you first. You're so much better about things like that. I thought you'd know one to suit him."

"To suit him...?" What suits a porcupine? But there was one just for him! "Quill."

"Quill? Yes. Yes, that's him!"

"Do you suppose he'll stay around the rest of the summer for us?"

"Oh, I hope so," she pleaded, almost beseeching the little creature through the glass panes and misty rain. "I want to get a good sketch of him. What should I have him doing, do you think? He's so cute. But he's not the domestic-type at all."

Cheek against the window I wondered about that. "Maybe he is, but in a growing up, exploring sort of way."

"Domesticated?" she challenged me, shocked.

"Not people-domesticated. Homebody-domesticated. More like considerate of his mother — and siblings. Things like that."

Annabel laughed, sitting back in her chair. She just looked at me as if I'd managed to turn into something as adorable as a drenched porcupine.

Adorable, memorable — a cherished sort of day it all turned into with cocoa, scones, and parlor stories about Quill. It was the beginning of our honesty with one another; we grew to respect each others' feelings and took much less for granted. And it was the day the stories about Quill began — the little critter who went wandering about in search of a place to make into a home of his own.

In that, he was a bit like the two of us.

The Fourth Summer
Chapter Four

I do wish I could wear those blue jeans."

Poking my head out of my walk-in closet, I just grinned at her.

Annabel grimaced and dropped onto the bed. She was clad rather comically in her high-necked, laced blouse and a green, too-short skirt that let yards of petticoat show.

"They fit you, why not?"

The grimace turned into a glare.

I laughed and disappeared back into the closet's depths.

My room, sunny and white with tall windows overlooking the lake, was never particularly neat. The old brass spyglass mounted in the south window echoed my love of brass and stained wood. Solid, well-worn things which bred security and respect for other generations were scattered about. A bookcase of scarred cherry, an ancient oak desk, a sprawling bed of brass and window seats with cushions of braided rags intermixed with white chest-of-drawers' and bric-a-brac shelves. It was a big and spacious room, with acoustics which would swell with music whether the sounds be from my guitar or stereo. But never-the-less, it was undeniably a mess of a room.

My stuffed animals were askew on the top of my cedar chest and half-hidden beneath clothes. Discarded shoes, hangers, and what-not littered the floor. This was not the first time Annabel and I had demolished a room, although it was the first time the room wasn't hers. It was my fourteenth birthday, Annabel was coming to my party — on my side of the lake! — and the room could have been hit by a tornado for all the thought I gave it now.

"Perfect!" I cried.

She brightened as I bounced back into the room.

"It's country, longer than fashion but really perfect for you. You'll feel comfortable in it, I promise! See?! It's even got a petticoat sewn in as part of it."

She spread the skirt I held, eyeing the denim with lace ruffles critically. Then slowly a delighted smile began to grow.

"Will it fit, you think?" I asked, suddenly a bit wary. We were nearly the same size because I was a bit taller. But between my skinny bones and her rounding hips, things were apt to hang a little differently here and there.

"Over my corset, certainly it should? Do let me try." She stripped the green atrocity away with her lacy underthings and took up the denim.

It always amazed me how easily she shimmied out of those petticoats and gartered stockings — although I imagine if I'd lived under Grandmama's tutelage for long, I'd acquire the knack as well. Then Annabel was sliding into the denim skirt, and I found myself grinning. I don't know if it was just her...or if that corset really did make the difference. But I'd certainly never looked that great in that skirt. The lace of her blouse accented the skirt's white inlays and hem, somehow charming all those ruffled frills into a comfortable, country style.

She fastened the buttons and did a pirouette for the mirror. "Its petticoat seems awfully flimsy—"

Annabel glanced at my plaid, yoked shirt and suddenly undid the pearl buttons of her cuffs and collar. Then adroitly, she rolled up the scratchy lace into three-quarter length sleeves.

"Well?"

I realized, I was grinning and staring. I pulled out a rueful growl instead. "You look better'n I ever did in it."

She stopped perching so anxiously on her toes, but pressed, "It's all right then?"

"Definitely."

"And shoes?"

The high-buttoned shoes she'd brought were laying about somewhere, but they were obviously not going to do.

"Sandals, I think!"

"Did you say you wanted me to do something with your hair?" she called as I rummaged through the closet again.

"That French braid thing — I'm so tired of pigtails."

She grinned mischievously as I came to stand before her, sandals in hand.

"Oh, I don't know. I kind of like them," and she tugged on one of my braids lightly.

"Stop it," I tried to scowl fiercely, "or I will make you wear blue jeans!"

I only made her laugh.

* * *

"Oh — no!"

"You all right?" I stuck my head around into the bathroom.

"No! I'm not. Help!" she pleaded. Annabel was sitting in the tub in a pile of frothy bubbles with one hand desperately holding her hair up and the other dripping with suds. "The pin slipped."

"Hang on!" I darted off.

Most of the west wing of the lodge was reserved for family. Mrs. Stevens had the back rooms downstairs across from the kitchen, and Uncle Jake had the back rooms upstairs with the staircase separating his from mine. But the length of the hallway held a linen cupboard that could have serviced a family of twelve. As it was, the extra odds'n'ends for the east wing guests filled a few shelves, and it was these supplies which I tore through.

Uncle Jake had always teased Mrs. Stevens for the number of disposable shower caps she kept on hand for the feminine clientele. He'd insist anyone coming to a fishing lodge wasn't the sort to be finicky about wet hair. Mrs. Stevens usually retorted that the men were the fishing fanatics and that the women, often as not, preferred doing their needlework projects or scouring the local antique shops, and they were just the type to appreciate a little civilized concern for niceties.

"Here—" I reappeared, my slippers squeaking on the damp floor.

"Thank heavens," she sat up a little straighter as I stuffed her curly locks into safety. "I almost thought you'd forgotten me."

"Never," I grinned. "Does that work?"

"Hmm-hmm," she smiled. "Thank you."

I pulled the vanity's stool away from the counter and sat, asking, "Is it my imagination or is your hair getting curlier by the year?"

She pulled a face and sank deeper into her bath. "I wish it were your imagination. And this lakeside air of yours only makes it worse."

"So unbearable," I teased, securing the belt of my cotton kimono as it slipped.

A toe reach up from the bubbly depths, and she opened the hot water tap for a second, sighing. "I feel completely decadent," she murmured. "Luxury does have its advantages."

"Well, even today there are still a lot of summer houses around here without electricity and stuff."

Annabel looked at me oddly as I propped a foot up on the edge of my stool. Then suddenly her brows lifted with amazement. "Jennifer Cassel! What are you doing?!"

I grinned, unabashed, "Painting my toenails."

"Why on earth?"

"Why not? Who sees'm but me?"

"Half the world I should think — considering how often you go swimming."

"They're not that bad," I protested and extended a foot for her inspection.

"Hmm—," was all the answer I got.

Less sure of myself, I examined my feet more critically. "Pearl isn't so awful. It's not like they're bright red or purple for cryin' out loud."

She giggled, amending, "But red would be so much more dramatic, don't you think?"

"Careful, Annabel," I murmured wickedly, "or you'll awaken with 'Flaming Tart' toes in the morning."

"You wouldn't be so cruel! Haven't I been through enough today for you?"

"Was it very awful?" I switched off the brattishness abruptly. I really had been concerned about her towards the end of the party. She had slipped off into the kitchens to help Mrs. Stevens, and I had been left wondering what was wrong.

"No, it was a wonderful party, Wren."

I looked at her for a moment.

"It was," she insisted, rising as she reached for

her towel. "I had a very nice time."

I sighed and played with the nail polish jar. "There were an awful lot of people."

"It was a family affair," she reminded me sensibly. "That usually means a lot of people."

Again I sighed. The barbecue had not just included my friends but their families as well. It was a sort of tradition we had since my birthday nearly marked the end of the summer season, and most of my local friends had parents or cousins who currently or in the past had worked at the lodge.

"Did you like your new boat?" Annabel asked softly, trying to find something to chase the melancholy from me.

"My canoe?" I had to brighten at that. "Isn't she beautiful? I can come visit you any old time I want to now. At least, as long as the water's relatively calm." I hesitated suddenly, remembering the white-faced horror that had struck Annabel as the old pick-up had driven in with my canoe. The bonfire had been roaring, Paul had been sitting next to her talking about something or other, and Mrs. Stevens' cousin, Jan Gregor, had come roaring down across the lawn — gravel flying as she hit the beach rocks — to deliver my "surprise."

"You will be careful, won't you?"

I blinked a little dumbfounded.

"When you're out boating?" she prompted, wrapping herself into a worn satin robe.

"Always am. And I swim, remember?"

She smiled fondly. "I wanted that model back so badly, and Dickie was being no help at all. Then you happened along, swimming much better than Dickie ever could."

"I was on my best form." I laughed a little,

"Showing off to get your attention, you know."

"Well, you got it. And I still think you're the better swimmer. Dickie can hardly keep his chin above water, showing off or not."

"And what about yourself?" I teased. "Are you ever going to let me teach you?"

"Another summer wasted." She laughed a little. "I do manage to avoid it, don't I?"

"We've still got a week. It's not too late to start this year—? You do keep pestering me about it every spring."

"That I do," she admitted and walked into the bedroom in search of her hair brush.

I did my teeth and followed after, turning off lights. In the bedroom I found it still dark, except for the bedside lamp. Annabel was standing beside the brass spyglass, gazing out into the night. She suddenly looked very alone, and I hesitated, joining her only slowly.

"Is that my house?" she asked quietly, pointing the brush towards the faint light across the lake.

There was no need for me look.

"Usually the place is hidden by the trees," I murmured. "But at night, Grandmama's study is sometimes lit and it sits above the tree line."

"The east canopy room... the one above the study? And the west one? If there were lights there, do you think you could see them too?"

"Probably," I swiveled the spyglass around and drew her back to see. The moon was bright and the house was dimly visible in the blue light of the night.

"It's so clear," she breathed, but I felt she was talking about something else.

"Sometimes," I admitted slowly. "Often it's hazy, especially in the morning when there's mist. Then I

can't see it at all."

"Do you try often?" She looked at me, expecting honesty.

"Yes." My mouth felt dry. "Especially before you've arrived. I kept hoping you might be a little early this year."

She smiled a bit. Then staring out into the night, her smile faded. "Mine is such a different world from yours."

I nodded, sinking my hands into my kimono's pockets as I knelt on the window seat.

"Do you know what Grandmama told me before we left this morning?"

Silently I shook my head, knowing Annabel didn't really need an answer. She was talking more to herself than to me.

"She said, things would seem very strange, but I shouldn't be afraid. She said to trust you and to trust myself... and that I needn't do anything if it felt uncomfortable."

Her paleness as she sat beside Paul came to me again, and I wondered if he'd done something. But Paul? Now if it'd been his older brother Brian, I wouldn't have been surprised. But Paul?

"I think, I did get a little overwhelmed," she mused, pushing aside the lace curtain as she stood, still gazing outward. "Too many strangers perhaps."

"But... I thought you were used to large gatherings," I ventured cautiously. "From all of Grandmama's artists and philanthropists—?"

"Large gatherings, yes — not so many strangers, though. Most drift in and out, slowly bringing new faces... " Then she roused a smile and turned to me. "I'm not saying I didn't have a good time, Wren."

I let her take my hands as she sank down onto

the window seat beside me.

"I did. Believe me, I did. Ever since my own birthday last March, I've been wishing so to be at your party — wishing you could have been there for mine."

"I wanted you here too."

"And you never neglected me," Annabel squeezed my hands, nearly reading my mind again. "Your friends are cheerful and wonderful. They made me feel welcomed, and when I grew tired I did something about it, Wren. I didn't need you to change anything, honestly."

"Is that why you ended up in the kitchen with Mrs. Stevens?"

"Yes," her cinnamon brown eyes caught mine. "Was that so terrible?"

"No," I grinned easily. "Mrs. Stevens likes you. She loved the help."

Annabel sat back, staring at the brush in her hands. "She knew, I think... that I needed a retreat for a bit. But — I never meant to hurt you, Wren."

"You didn't," I took my turn in reassuring her. "You even looked like you were having fun, the times I checked in on you."

"I was," she laughed. "Her stove is absolutely marvelous. I was in seventh heaven doing tomorrow's bread baking with her."

"That old wood burner?" I shook my head in amazement. "It's the only thing she insisted on keeping for the kitchen when Uncle Jake took over and remodeled. It was originally from her grandmother's inn down the south end of the lake. She says nothing cooks so well as a good hot fire and as long as she's here it'll be the only thing this place ever uses."

"But I've never seen one so big — it's the length of that whole wall!"

"Well, we do have quite a few mouths to feed around here in the summer."

"I can imagine." Her gaze drifted back to the shining, moonlit lake.

I watched her, wondering what she was thinking. Wondering too just how overwhelmed she had come to feel. I bit my lip and asked, "Do you think you might like to come again sometime?"

She smiled and nodded, eyes pinned to the faint glow of home across the lake. Then she shared, "I've never been away from family overnight. Not since—"

My hand touched hers gently.

"... Not since my parents died. Then it was only the once, and Dickie was there. I barely even remember it. I only knew I was frightened — so very frightened. Because I knew, nothing was ever going to be the same again."

I was quiet a moment, watching her pensive face. And then, I offered, "Would you like to go home, Annabel?"

"No," she shook her head faintly, before turning to me. "It's strange, but I don't feel so very far from home here. Not with you here. And yet...." Her voice drifted away with her gaze.

I tugged encouragingly on her hands.

"Wren," she came back to me, "it's almost that same feeling all over again."

"Being frightened?"

"No. No, the feeling — like nothing's ever going to be quite the same."

I tightened my grasp and then hugged her. There didn't seem to be anything I could say to that.

The Fifth Summer
Chapter Five

I never knew sunsets could be so beautiful," Annabel murmured.

A mere nod was all I managed. It was indeed a special place to be at sundown, near this lake of mine.

We sat companionably on the bench at her dock's end, listening to the water lap beneath our feet and watching the colors glide amidst the silver and sapphire waters. So calm, so smooth, and yet so alive with hues of rose and amber. The boathouse hid the sinking red globe now, as the western sky glowed and strewed rippling ribbons of light across the lake. In the northeast, the indigo sky of night was already deepening, and the breeze was the barest brush of coolness against our cheeks.

"Twilight is never so peaceful at home," and again she spoke so softly that nothing about us was disturbed.

The lake's surface broke with the flop of a fishtail, then the small thing was gone. The criek-up croak of the lake frogs joined the crickets' cheek-et sounds. A bird called from somewhere to nowhere, and the lake grew grayer as the colors ebbed.

"It's this lake," I stirred, my words pitched as quietly as hers had been. "If I sit still long enough, no matter what I'm doing — or feeling, it reaches in and touches me. It can be stormy with white caps or quiet like this — it doesn't matter. It's always here, always steady... always beautiful."

Her gaze fell to me and I felt her long, measuring review. I knew without turning that I could find my lake's serenity — its steadiness in her eyes too. I smiled faintly, breathing in the sweet peace, and watched the lake darken.

Her skirts rustled as Annabel turned towards me more, settling back into the sculpted, wooden bench. She had changed so much and yet so little in these past winter months. Seemingly older than I at times — she already fifteen, while my own birthday was still to come in a month — and yet my cherished playmate often reappeared unexpectedly, startling me with a comical remark or girlish delight in the passing moment. She had exchanged the hair ribbons for pins, and amber gold had replaced the mousy brown tresses of last summer. Her skirts had lengthened to below her ankles, blouses long-sleeved and cuffed with simple lace. Her skin, always clear, had lost even its occasional blotchiness, and the pink that touched her cheeks was wholly her own.

There were times I felt amazingly clumsy, almost gauche, next to her. I was too skinny, still without a hint of a bust blooming, my skin broke out regardless of the chocolate that I ate (or didn't eat), and there was no reason I could see for wanting to hurry and grow-up. Except that there was, of course. All the things she gently reminded me of with her very presence, I was sorely aware of at school. Uncle Jake reminded me that coming up on the tenth grade was still young for obsessive dating interests; Mrs. Stevens clucked her tongue and maintained everybody does their growing in their own good time, and I felt less pressured by the whole dominating escapade of adolescence.

So, I would sit myself down and be still for a time, letting the beauty of my lake seep nearer and nearer until I felt at one with it. It was then I'd find, the whole meddlesome world moved slowly towards its proper place — which changed the importance of much.

"Is it the lake you see?" Annabel mumbled reflectively.

I looked at her, waiting.

"The peace that settles about you is so...?" she struggled for words, her eyes leaving me. "I can feel it, it's so strong. Steady, I think you'd say.

"You absorb it." Her words came slowly as I gazed back to the waters. "I feel the calm, but you — you merge with it. You share the quiet, the strength. Then you pass it on to me — or to your uncle or Grandmama—. It's such a wonderful gift you bring us. Yet, is it merely because of this place, I wonder?"

My breath released. Almost unconsciously, I'd been holding it — holding on to the scent of twilight, that magical moment of neither day nor night when all things blur beneath the fading light and yet seem clearer, equal in their station.

"I think it's more," Annabel answered herself, her voice growing even quieter. "I think... maybe this is the way you pray."

The sureness... the completeness that filled me with the evening's descent accepted her comment and meshed it gently into the whole. I found myself smiling and admitted, "I think maybe you're right."

She was still a moment more. Then she shifted to slip an elbow over the bench back and put her chin down on her forearm. Patient, she simply waited for me to say more.

"Religion has never been particularly attractive to me," I finally began. "The world has been full of too many senseless wanderings for me — to many senseless faces. I've seen some play with money so carelessly, while a stone's throw away there are others going hungry on the alley streets. Yet then there come moments... moments when the nuns talk, or Jake sighs, or when I see some stranger offering help to an old couple in a grocery store.... At moments like those, everything seems to make an odd sort of sense. So maybe there is a higher source — a kindly source, I hope, who is watching and wishing us well. All the time we waste, tying ourselves into knots of convention and social expectations...?" A sigh passed my lips. "Perhaps the helpless knots we create for ourselves, bind those benevolent hands as well? When we let go and simply accept what is, maybe then we free — well, maybe then each of us can see how best to live in just being ourselves... or whatever. I don't know."

"No—" she countered gently, "I think you do know."

At my questioning look, Annabel straightened and waved outwards at the water and the ring of dark hills about the lake basin. "At least, here you do."

And then it was her turn to sigh. "I hear so many versions of right and wrong, morality and justice — so many people stirring their neighbors with convictions of what must be. Grandmama's parlor is filled with them. All of them so certain — all so clear in their truth.

"And yet they search so, Wren. Did you know that Grandmama's family loyalties were divided — still are divided — because some remained Catholics while others chose to be Huguenots? Yet so often, she has no answers for me — through all those strife-ridden, embittered years, was nothing more unveiled?

"In Philadelphia, it seems no different. In our parlor, the names of the factions change, but the confusion remains. Always impassioned, always driven...." Her clear gaze returned to me, "Why? Is the truth something to be browbeaten into others? Has it no strength of its own? They espouse capitalism over anarchism! Immaculate Conception over blasphemy! How Darwin's destiny is proof for imperialism! Such ideals, all bandied about yet they fall so flat when day fades and night comes. And I wonder if answers are truth or if perhaps truth is something less rational? Something less tangible in some way?"

I thought about that, the wholeness of the country surrounding me.

"And then I see you. Standing in the rain at the end of the dock, warming — glowing even in the cold dampness. I see you digging in the garden, your hands almost tender in the way you smooth the soil aside. I see you here — watching the day draw to a close. And I see something I can believe in, something I — if I'm very still, I can almost feel this calmness of yours approach me."

I nodded faintly. "Praying is a good word for it, Annabel."

She nodded too. "Spiritual is not always religious, Grandmama is often saying. I think I begin to grasp a little of what she means."

With a smile, I took her hand in both of mine. "Then welcome home."

"Yes," she took in the shadows and silhouettes of the night. "It is like coming home. It's like being folded into a cherished embrace."

"Like the love of the mother both of us have missed for long," I added.

"Mother?" She paused, then nodded again as pieces fell into place for her. "The Greeks said all came from the mother's womb of the Earth."

I shrugged. "Even the nuns at the Academy honor the Mother of God."

"Strange," and her lips curled in a fond, faraway smile, "how things go in circles."

"Like the seasons," I murmured, gazing up as the stars began to appear. The black velvet sky above, the black satin waters below — all dusted with silver sparkle.

Annabel's grasp tightened in mine. She understood.

* * *

In many ways, that summer passed uneventfully for us. Still in other respects, it was so very important, because it was the year we choose a measured silence — to preserve the joy of our friendship. Yet it was also the first time we let any silence tear the joy from our trust.

Annabel's painting developed. My music fumbled along, but I was beginning to write now as Annabel encouraged me to put down the playful stories of Quill and his small garden adventures. Although the prickly fellow himself was no longer around, we still amused ourselves on rainy days with tales of his whereabouts. (In wintry Chicago I had often found myself spinning tales of him for the neighborhood children as I baby-sat.) We laughed together over Grandmama's day maid, Sally, as we inadvertently spied her stealing a kiss from her local beau, we came to tears over Romeo and Juliet as we revisited Shakespeare — and Grandmama taught us how to waltz properly.

I finally — reluctantly — learned to wear corsets and lace-throated blouses as I joined the odd formal dinners for Grandmama's visiting acquaintances. And I respectfully learned to hide my humor, at the seances her assorted guests inevitably arranged. Except, of course, during those moments when Annabel would catch my eye, and then we'd share a somewhat giddy smile.

In her turn, Annabel visited me, and Mrs. Stevens taught her how to use shortening instead of lard to make pie crusts. I introduced her to Kotex instead of bulkier rags (and thereafter did my best to supply her with enough to be comfortable through the winter in Philadelphia). We canned preserves and jellies, sputtered on brandy-laced coffee (after raiding Uncle Jake's liquor cabinet), and dangled bare feet in the lake's coolness as we philosophized.

Why I would fret at wearing corsets or why she had never learned of Kotex, were something we only tentatively challenged each other to explain. Because although we'd learned to respect our differences over the past summers, those differences were beginning to stand out more and more.

All along it had been the little things which had made no sense. Like when I gave Annabel a book of sonnets by Longfellow and the copyright page made her frown; Grandmama shrugged it aside as a misprint. Or like Grandmama's refusal to give me the postal address of their summer house. Although many summer residents at Chautauqua used boats as often as cars, the awkwardness of always coming across the lake rather than using the road began to seem very odd to me. So time and again, Annabel and I found ourselves taking questions to Grandmama — only to be gently rebuked for dwelling overmuch on the differences between our families' worlds and in so doing, taking the blessings of our friendship for granted. But still curiosity prodded, and we'd press her for more. Until finally, one day early in that fifth summer, Grandmama's patience snapped.

"Do you care for each other?!"

Numbly, we could only nod, the sharpness in her retort catching us both by surprise. Then, suddenly — fearfully — we began to grasp there was a great importance behind whatever she was refusing to tell us.

"Then respect your differences for what they are — simply a part of your lives!" Grandmama studied us gravely, the sternness hardening in her words as she continued. "You each have bright, curious minds, and it is not a bad thing to cultivate the intellect. But common sense and science will never account for all we find in life. And there are times, when taking a relationship so much for granted that you pry apart each piece of each day to examine the how and why of it all, only leads to the discovery that the relationship itself ultimately must suffer and be lost."

After that day, no further inquiries were condoned.

As for the questions Annabel and I still found before us? We sought no refute of any kind for Grandmama's silence, and obviously quit our occasional approach to Uncle Jake or Mrs. Hodges as well. Given the joy Annabel and I held so preciously within our friendship...? Given our past loss of parents...? Well, we were too intimately acquainted with the frailty of life's gifts. It's not surprising that neither Annabel nor I ever wanted to challenge anyone again for answers. When weighed against the risk of losing each other, even the oddest of our differences became trivial.

Since over our summers together, we had grown close, in the ways sisters can be close, it really wasn't so hard to shrug aside the anomalies. As it was, I came more to dread the winters when Annabel was not about. I caught myself incessantly wondering, if she would approve of a new Quill story. Or I'd find myself waiting excitedly for summer, when I could boast of the date to a spring dance with the basketball star. (Tomboy or no — Uncle Jake used to say I was a handful at any party, hence the dance committees and drama clubs knew me well.) But somehow, everything I ever did at school seemed less alive — less bright — than any single, summer day I could share with Annabel.

And that summer... with its painting and music and writing, with flour fights in Mrs. Stevens' kitchen and restrained giggles in Grandmama's seances... to me, it seemed that summer was nearly the most wonderful we'd ever share — until its last day.

The day was in the last week of Annabel's summer stay. It was in the week after my fifteenth birthday. It was a dismal day of cruelty. It was the day she told me we'd have no summer in the next year.

"You see, Wren, Dickie finishes school this spring, and — well, I'll be turning sixteen which seems quite the proper age to be presented to Society. So Grandmama has arranged for us to travel to London, where we'll meet Dickie and cousin Edward — and the London Society. She — well she says, I'll even be among those presented to Queen Victoria." I didn't say a word, and she stammered on with an effort. "Th-then later during the summer, Grandmama proposes we visit the rest of our — more distant relations. I believe, we're to see Edward's people in Amsterdam first and then later Grandmama's own in Brugg."

We were sitting on the verandah, sharing tea, but the humid, summer afternoon went cold around me. And suddenly, deep in the pit of my stomach, I felt like something died. With a shaking hand, I managed to set down my biscuit. Annabel shifted awkwardly, the wicker chair creaking faintly around her. It was a weak, little sound that only made the sudden silence between us more pronounced. I could only sit there, stupidly noticing I'd lost my napkin again and yet still needed to dust the powder sugar from my fingers.

"I — I don't particularly want to go," Annabel's voice held a forced lightness in its tone. "Still, it seems necessary. After all, someday Edward will take over the Boston offices, just as Dickie is to do in New York. And well, it might be advantageous for me to know him — Edward — a bit before he moves to America — and for his family to become acquainted with me as well. And of course, it is something of an honor to be in London with the Queen—"

"Victoria isn't Queen anymore," I bit out harshly. "Elizabeth is."

Her gaze dropped as the silence descended.

But the silence no longer let us hide, and I could only feel the betrayal of loss. All of Grandmama's reprimands — all of the differences — it wasn't fair!!! Grandmama should have told us — why and how and — and how to fight against losing each other! Yet now there was only Annabel's duties in Grandmama's time of old Boston and New York... and in their old world where Richard was becoming the grown man readying to claim his powers over Business and Family.

She should have told us. Grandmama should have told us! All those platitudes about not prying into every little thing because we might lose the very thing we cherished the most — our time together! Until now! Now when it would happen anyway!!!

"Jenny...?" Annabel touched my wrist tentatively.

"She lied to us!" I pulled away from her, scraping the chair back and jumping to my feet in a burst of panic. "Grandmama lied to us! We can't be friends simply by ignoring all the differences. By ignoring it's Time itself we can't share!!"

"Wren don't do this. Please don't do this?!"

"I'm not doing anything! I can't do anything! You can't. I can't. Nothing we do can! It doesn't matter we care for each other. You're still leaving! Don't you see?! Caring isn't enough. Friendship by itself will never be enough. It isn't going to make you come back next summer—"

The words failed me abruptly as our eyes met, and yes, we both understood there would be no summer next year. But worse, came the realization of the brevity all our summers held in and of themselves. This trip to Europe next year, it was simply the beginning. Someday — someday there would never be another summer of any kind to share with Annabel.

"No." Annabel's protest was quiet and forceful. "No. Caring will be enough, Jenny. We can make it enough. No matter what or how Time slips and toys with us, we—"

"Stop it, Annabel," and the fight had left me completely now. "Neither of us are twelve and naively eating apples on the tree limbs anymore. Even Quill has moved on."

"But—" her voice trembled in its plea for belief... for reassurance, "I'll be gone only for the one summer. Wren — please?"

In a single instant, the helpless — uselessness of such promises took me back to the black rainy day in Chicago — to all the emptiness of the winter in

Amsterdam.

"Europe is a fine place," I said quietly, a numbing ice growing within me to distance us even further. "I'm sure you'll enjoy your travels."

Then I turned to walk away, thinking it was well I'd brought myself over in my canoe that day; there would be no need to wait for any prearranged rendezvous with a guide from the lodge. There was no need to wait for anything... and so I left Annabel there on the big, sprawling porch of that old, Victorian house. I left her alone while I took myself home, where I stayed.

I didn't return again that week, not even to say good-bye.

The Seventh Summer
Chapter Six

There are a great many days which go into making twenty-two-and-a-half months. I'll admit I didn't fret over my foolishness every hour of every one of those many days, but it would be a lie to say I didn't regret it. I did, acutely. It would also be a lie to say I assumed Annabel would simply forgive me in exchange for some pious apology. I had hurt her, badly. Just how badly...? I agonized over that almost nightly.

So I waited. Through the hectic turmoil of a sophomore's high school year, through the aching beauty of a summer without her — through another year of nuns, socials and academia, I waited for spring to waken again. Until finally, June came. With an immense sense of relief and even a hint of triumph, I returned home to Jake and the lodge. But the joy was short-lived. As July finally, begrudgingly arrived, Annabel did not.

I began to fear she would not be returning at all.

Desperation would have sent me across the lake nearly every day in search of hope against hope, but I had left it 'til too late, and the season was well and truly open. On occasion, I found myself regretting my assertion to Uncle Jake that I wanted to 'grow-up' and join him in running the fishing lodge instead of entering business or academia. Although on the whole, my new duties kept me busy enough to curb my anxieties. I made myself content with a slow trawl for fish off her shore — the fishermen keeping me boat-bound. Yet the dilapidated remains of a rotted-apart dock was all I ever found; the neatly stained, L-shaped dock with its lantern poles and bench remained absent. And so I knew she'd not returned.

In the evening, I'd then turn my brass spyglass towards the Victorian turrets, only to sigh with gnawing impatience.

To say good-bye to a friend is one thing. To turn your back on her is quite another. I didn't like the feeling.

* * *

The evening sky was gathering with gloom, forecasting a sizable thunderstorm to be followed by a light drizzle for a day or two. Reasonably good weather for fishing and our Cleveland folks had been in good cheer around the dinner table that night.

Uncle Jake was still out with his sunset group, although they'd be back by the first downpour. I'd sent the other guides home for the night. Mrs. Stevens was downstairs sewing with her ear tuned to the short-wave in case Jake called for a little help. In all the years he'd owned the lodge, the radio had never been used except to announce in-coming frozen hands in desperate need of hot coffee. But safety was worth the extra mile and I always agreed with him on that.

All in all, it was the type of night I dreaded — all that quiet before the storm. It always made me restless as I wondered if my loved ones would come home safe — it had been raining that day in Chicago when mother hadn't. Mrs. Stevens was accounted for, Jake was nearly a sure thing... yet tonight Annabel's absence came to haunt me as well.

The old Victorian skeleton leered back at me, her glowing yellow eyes taunting me above those faraway trees. Worry all I might, she would lend no comfort tonight.

I almost turned away, a hand already unbuttoning my flannel shirt.

Then I stared harder. Yellow eyes of welcome, not mockery! A smile grew on my lips as I recognized the faint glow of lamplight in the upper rooms. Annabel had lit both east and west corners; there was no mistake about it.

Swallowing hard, I reminded myself of duties. I wasn't free to go flying off on a whim. I needed to wait at least until Jake was in. But if I was ready, I might just be able to slip over and back between his return and the storm's arrival. Time and transport wouldn't be a problem as I had my own motorboat now, but my welcome?

I left the window to unlock my desk. From inside I lifted a small jewelry box, its lid carved with roses and vines. Opening it, I gently touched the locket within, the rose and vine design was identical to the box. I'd had the carvings done to match the gold when I'd found the locket during those last winter months. I knew without looking what the locket's inscription read... so very simply, it said — friends.

I shut the box gently, wondering if we were.

* * *

I left the canvas half-secured over my boat as I tied her to the dock. A steady drizzle had begun while I was mid-way across the lake, but as long as the thunder wasn't rolling, I knew I had time. That thought only caused me to hesitate, however. It was nearly ten o'clock, and it suddenly occurred to me, this was not exactly the most neighborly of times to come calling.

Grandmama would be in bed. But what on earth was I going to say to Mrs. Hodges?

The tempo of the rain changed and sent me forward. The downpour had my shoes soaking, and my blue jeans from the knees down were wringing wet. I was certainly not much of a house guest, and before I could lose my nerve, I rapped on the door. Light from the stairway sconces glimmered through the etched windows, but there was no sign of any movement within. I found myself pounding again.

An oil lamp lit in the recesses of the dining room. Resigned but none-the-less nervous, I stepped back to shake the water from my poncho. I had asked for this.

"Who's there?" Mrs. Hodges' voice was unmistakable.

"It's me, Mrs. Hodges. Jennifer Cassel!"

"Who?" The latch was fumbling a bit.

"Jennifer Cassel — Jenny, from across the lake."

"Why — dear?!" A most astonished housekeeper opened the door to me. "Miss, you're — but come in. Come in!"

The door rattled shut behind us and I half pulled my hood back rather sheepishly, "I apologize for the late hour, Mrs. Hodges. But I saw your lights from across the way and just wanted to make sure you had everything ready for the storm and such — "

"Mrs. Hodges?"

I faltered at the sound of her voice and turned as a figure moved out from the shadows of the upper staircase. Hair loose and shawl clutched about her shoulders, Annabel appeared in a flannel nightgown carrying a chamber stick high. I thought again, I must be crazy to have intruded.

"Wren!"

Thunder struck somewhere, breaking her astonished stillness, and Annabel hurried forward as Mrs. Hodges broke out with, "It's Miss Jenny, Miss. She's come all the way out in this weather to see if'n we're well settled. Says she saw our house lights'n—"

"In this weather, Jenny?" Annabel stood very near, worry creasing her forehead, and lightning cracked outside with enough violence to make Mrs. Hodges jump; I don't think either Annabel or I heard it properly. "I didn't mean for you to risk tonight, Wren."

It was almost a plea the way she whispered it, and I suddenly felt the breath sweep into me again. She had meant for me to see the lights.

Another thunderbolt cracked and I pulled myself together. I did need to get out of here. "I just came to see that you were well."

Annabel forestalled me with a firm shake of her head, "Don't imagine you can go back out in this. Mrs. Hodges, put the kettle on. Miss Jenny is spending the night with us, and I believe a good hot drink is in order."

"Yes, Miss. Oh, but Miss," Mrs. Hodges looked crestfallen as she realized, "the spare linens aren't aired yet Miss. I've naught to—"

"Don't trouble yourself, Mrs. Hodges. She can sleep with me as usual," Annabel's dimpled smile turned to me. "We're apt to be up talking most of the night, I expect. There's quite a lot of time we've to cover—"

"But I can't—"

"That you both do, Miss," and Mrs. Hodges patted my shoulder fondly. "It's good to see you again, Miss Jenny."

"But I need—"

"Just leave the kettle on, Mrs. Hodges. I'll see to the tea myself. You run along and find some sleep. It's been a long day for all of us."

"Aye, good-night to the two of you."

"But my boat!" I hissed, finally catching Annabel's full attention.

"What about it?"

"It's — I — " Lightning flashed and thunder clipped its heels, interrupting me with a finality her words could never have carried. There was no way I could safely cross again tonight. Out on that lake I'd be a sitting duck for every lightning bolt in the county.

"Please don't try, Wren."

I sighed, thrust the package at her that I'd been keeping hidden beneath my poncho and jerked the rubber hood up over my head again. "I need to secure the canvas and make sure of the knots."

She nodded with an encouraging smile. "Do be careful."

"Yeah," I grinned, suddenly realizing that I was going to be spending another twelve whole hours with her, "count on it."

* * *

There was a brief knock on the bedroom door, and I glanced up from my place at the fire as Annabel appeared with the largest of tea trays. Smiling, I curled my toes back under my flannel nightie and gave-up toweling my hair dry.

"Is that real food?" I asked in awe, wondering at this knack she still had — after nearly two years — of reading my mind.

She laughed and set the tray on the hearth, settling herself down on the rug a few feet from me.

"How did you know?" and I snatched up a cold meat sandwich, sighing in pleasure as her homemade bread literally melted in my mouth. Heavens, how many times had I sworn I'd imagined that sweet taste? I paused and gave her a sheepish, "Thank you."

"You're welcome," and she seemed only too happy to simply watch me.

I took the tea she offered, snuggling myself deeper into the afghan as I lent back against the foot of the armchair. From the corner of my eye, I noticed Annabel doing the same, her tea in hand and the smallest of smiles playing across her mouth.

"I like it," she murmured finally.

Startled, I turned. "Like what?"

"Your hair. You've cut it."

I had. Self-consciously I ran my fingers through the damp mess, trying for some semblance of order. "It's still pretty long — feathers down past my shoulders."

"I said I like it."

I smiled, and sandwich finished, hid my face in my tea.

"Would you like something more?" she inquired politely, but her words were laced with amusement.

"Another cup would be nice." Damn if we weren't beginning to sound formal.

But her fingers were warm as they touched mine, handing the tea back to me. I found myself smiling all over again.

It was a ridiculous feeling to be so happy over absolutely nothing.

Except, of course, there was something — there was us.

"I've missed you," I mumbled, staring into the depths of my teacup. "I wanted to apologize for walking off like that. It wasn't very nice of me. You didn't deserve it."

"I've missed you too... and the blame is mine to share."

A little self-irony mixed with my disbelief, "I doubt it."

"No," Annabel insisted quietly, staring into the crackling fire. "I was afraid you'd leave and — forget me... that you'd assume I'd never be back. I had known for most of the summer that the trip was a possibility, but I was so frightened of — of being carted off to Europe like some horse to auction I just couldn't bear to think about it, let alone talk. I knew — somehow — that all along Dickie was hoping not to bring me back... hoping I'd stay in Amsterdam with Edward. It was frightening to think I had such little say in my own future. I realize now, it wasn't so much that I was afraid you would assume I'd disappear, as it was my own worst fear that I might."

I sat quietly for the longest time, wondering if those were tears gathering in the corners of her eyes. But she wouldn't look at me.

"Was it so bad?" I ventured gently. "Europe—? Edward?"

"Europe, no," she almost shook her head, but then she grew paler and still. "Edward, yes."

Abruptly Annabel pulled herself back from her memories, forestalling my questions with, "I'll tell you of him another time, all right?"

I hesitated, then nodded. "All right."

She didn't quite smile, and I suddenly realized there was something I could do about this helpless feeling inside of me — I could listen. Whenever she was ready, I could simply listen.

"Annabel, I'm sorry I wasn't there when you

needed me—"

She turned away again, allowing, "It was a difficult situation."

"It was petty and childish of me," I corrected firmly and reached across, catching her chin in my hand, "and I'm sorry."

With heartfelt honesty I held her gaze, and finally the tension in her melted. A smile grew as she took my hand from her face, "Thank you."

I grinned, squeezing her fingertips and bounded up to fetch my package where she'd left it on the bedside table.

"This is for you."

The brown paper was damp, but the tissue beneath glowed with its warm yellow color. She was careful in the unwrapping, loath to tear the paper, and I remembered this was how she always opened presents.

"Oh — !" Her fingers caressed the dark, rich wood with its carvings. "Wren, it's beau—" She hushed as the lid lifted, the gold locket glittering faintly in the fire's light.

"Inside," I prompted quietly.

The locket's latch released, and I held my breath, waiting for an eternity.

Her smile deepened as her eyes misted, and she drew me near to kiss my cheek.

"Oh yes, Wren — for always and always." Her forehead tipped to mine — her fingers gentle against the nape of my neck, and I found we were both crying. "Thank you."

She moved away to place the chain around her neck, and I held the box as she fastened the catch.

"It's so lovely." She turned the little gold disk over and over in her hand, as if unable to believe it was real. Then suddenly, "I have something for you too—"

She was back in an instant with a small portfolio.

"I hope...?" She waved her words aside and then sat with her hands clenched tightly in her lap, "Just open it."

Curiously, I did and felt my mouth drop in amazement.

"Do you remember him?"

"Quill—" I breathed, spellbound by the splashes of color and ink which filled the pages before me. And suddenly, eagerly my fingers turned the storybook pages. My words she had turned into art... some watercolors, some ink sketches — all beautiful as they followed the young wanderer on his lost journey — and then home. The sunsets and gardens, the moles and muskrats... his clumsy encounters with clams and kitty-cats, it was all there.

"Do you like them?"

"Like them?" I echoed and stared at her in confusion. "How could anyone not like them?"

She relaxed, glowing in pleasure.

"They're incredible... absolutely incredible." And I found myself transported back to those rainy days in the parlor as I leafed through them again. "They must have taken you forever to do."

"Not really," she shrugged. I just stared at her, and disconcerted she pulled her shawl around her a bit as she began to blush.

"Why—?" I swallowed hard and shook my head at a loss.

"I did them on the boat mostly. I—" she shrugged again. "It made me feel safer — less stranded from home to remember his antics whether real or imagined. And then you'd feel closer, so I did them for you."

"They're beautiful, Annabel. I can't tell you how — thank you. Thank you so much."

"Thank you — for coming tonight," and the warmth of her voice made my heart sing. "I didn't mean you to, not in this storm. But I am glad you're here."

"So am I. Part of me was afraid you wouldn't be coming this summer. It's been such a long time—?"

"It has," and I recognized that familiar, practical sort of tone she had. "Now, you're to tell me everything. What have you been doing in school? Are you still in school—?"

I laughed and nodded, "For better or worse, I am—"

"... So your father still doesn't approve of his brother, Jake?"

"Not at all. He has no patience for quiet, empty days and wasted time. And he sees Jake's life as nothing but that — wasted time."

"Then how are you going to manage the partnership? Financially, I mean?"

"It's not such a problem. My Mother's money was left to me in a trust. When I'm eighteen it will be mine to do with as I please. So if I still feel the same come twenty, Uncle Jake will sign me on permanently. It won't matter what Father has to say."

"Was she well off then? Your mother?"

"Very. Socially, it was considered quite a match between the families when she married Father. Although I never exactly understood why she..."

"...it was all quite frustrating to have my painting treated as if it were some child's nursery game. I felt as you must when your father belittles your music — or your writing."

"It is maddening to have something so central in your life dismissed so easily."

"It's demeaning! I do not want to be treated as if my only worthy function revolves around child care and... "

"... a bit. A professor Donavan at Father's university has taken an interest in my writing, especially in my the children's stories... "

"... education can be threatening."

"Dickie was appalled! Absolutely appalled at my ability to discuss art and history — and to think. But how could he expect me to run a household the size of Grandmama's, if I'm not intelligent enough to balance an account? Then he acts as if I've disgraced the entire family by following his meagerly discourse on government budgets and economics? I say, it's virtually the same although on a larger scale. Except, of course," and she smiled, "temper tantrums within one's staff are certainly easier to resolve than those between Trade Unionists and Socialists—"

"—never really envied you that freedom."

"I'm not so sure I do myself. I mean, Paul's nice, and he writes faithfully during the winter, so it's convenient — at school, I mean. The girls just assume I've got this out-of-town sweetheart and don't expect much more than a lukewarm romance between me and anybody else I might meet."

"And is he, Wren?"

"Is he what?"

"Your sweetheart."

I paused, a knot tying tight in my chest as I faced something I'd been trying to avoid for nearly a year. "No."

"You don't sound pleased."

"I think... there's something wrong with me."

Annabel slipped her arm through mine, giving me a reassuring hug. "What's wrong?"

"I don't know," and I found it easier to stare into the fire.

"Know what?"

"It's different — what I have with Paul. It's not the same as what the other girls talk about. There's no... fire... or spark. He's sweet. That's how I think of him. Sweet... I like him. No, in my own way I do love him. Just as in his way he loves me. But it's a quiet sort of — brotherly love, Annabel. We talk about the boat motors he's repairing, about the mess Uncle Jake makes with the new account forms — about the best fishing holes. We don't talk about dreams or together-always sorts of things. When he visited up in Chicago, we played tourist and did all the things you do with your friends to introduce him around, you know. But it's not — real. He doesn't try to kiss me when we're alone — or even allude to it. And we're alone a lot between the nights we were unchaperoned at my father's house and the days we're in the barn sanding down the hulls together."

"Do you want him to kiss you?"

"It'd be a lie to say yes."

"But you have anyway?"

I nodded. "We do. When I think about it, we must fairly often. Whenever we go somewhere in the evenings or do anything resembling a 'romantic' outing, he'll kiss me good-night or good-bye or whatever. It's not unpleasant but... even when I'm thinking I'd like him to — even if I'm the one to initiate it... it's empty."

"Perhaps he's simply not the right man for you?"

I shrugged.

She peered at me, sensing my reluctance. "You said you love him?"

I nodded bleakly. "He's kind, sensitive, good-looking, and — well, he's always willing to talk." I smiled a bit crookedly at that. "I don't think I would have managed last summer without him to listen... with you being gone."

"But now?"

"It's just, I've felt more for him than I ever imagined I could feel for a fellow and yet, there's something — wrong. Something's not there. And it scares me sometimes. You know, I'm going to be a senior in high school, and I still feel like I've never been properly kissed?!"

She hid a smile, or tried to, and I found myself laughing with her. "I sound pretty pathetic, don't I?"

"No," Annabel squeezed my hand, serious again. "You sound... confused. Maybe a bit frightened?"

I hung onto her hand tightly, blinking back unsteady tears as I gazed into the fire. "Yeah, I guess I am."

She was quiet a while, just staying close. I felt a little less lost with her near.

Then, "Have you ever...?" she hesitated, moistening her lips as she rethought her comment, until finally, she began again. "In Philadelphia — or rather, in Grandmama's parlor — there are quite a lot of people with different perspectives and lifestyles."

I watched her, listening.

"Could it be you... I mean, I don't really know what kind of exposure you've had to different lives or values since — since you began your Catholic schooling, Wren. But, well there are women I've met among Grandmama's friends who... don't care for men at all..."

"You mean, women who love other women?"

"Yes." She ventured a cautious look at me, and I suddenly felt a bit dense. I nodded, frowning. Sometimes I can be very slow in my self-discovery, and I wondered why the thought had never occurred to me before.

"You may be right," I admitted. "I don't think I know yet."

Her grasp tightened on mine, and she was concerned at my withdrawal. "It doesn't mean something's wrong with you, Wren. No matter what you find, neither way is wrong. They're just different..." and there was almost a note of pleading in her voice.

"You honestly believe that?" I murmured, desperately hoping she did. I didn't want to lose her friendship just because of what I might or might not be. At that moment, above all else, losing Annabel was the worst fate I could imagine.

"Yes, I do." Her cinnamon eyes held mine steadily. "Believe me, I do."

Chapter Seven

The kitchen door to the dining room was propped open, urging the mid-morning breezes to cool the place down as the oven threatened to bake more than the bread. The smell of fresh strawberry tarts and scones mingled with the yeasty scent of dough, and I felt my mouth water as I paused in the doorway.

Clad in a long, blue skirt and an apron, Annabel stood behind the sprawling butcher block table kneading the dough into submission. As I watched, she divided the mound in two, tucking the edges under, and then setting the pair of loaves aside to rise again she turned to the next reluctant lump. Her face was smudged with flour and set with concentration, but there was an air of contentment to her and not the faintest trace of a frown marred her features.

"Did you know," I began softly, and she looked up in surprise, "the word for lady comes from an Old English root meaning breadkneader?"

An amused, tolerant sort of smile invited me in as she shook her head at me.

"I never quite understood that," I grinned, "until now. As I watch you making bread, I can see how much care and love you fold into each loaf."

She was laughing at me now as she wiped her hands on the tea towel. "There are those among Grandmama's more radical acquaintances who would scorn me for such 'nurturing nonsense.' They would have me out marching for reforms or at least painting for posterity."

"Well, doesn't someone have to feed posterity?"

Her head tilted a bit, and her laughter faded. "You really don't mind me liking such nonsense as cooking and cleaning."

"You neither cook nor clean," I corrected, facing her squarely. "You create a sense of home — of belonging that includes family and visitors alike. There is as much art to that as to your sketches and watercolors, and I find nothing at all nonsensical in any of it."

She laughed, flattered this time, and waved to the rising loaves, "Second batch goes in soon. I made extra for you, if you can stay 'til they're through?"

I grinned, "Tempt me."

"How about some lunch? Soup with the best of Grandmama's garden vegetables and cold, sliced beef? I'll even make you one of your atrocious sandwiches?"

"With fresh bread?"

"And brown mustard with apricot jam."

She did know my weaknesses. "Let them wait for the old motor parts — I'm yours for two hours!"

"Then make yourself useful and squeeze us some lemonade, while I finish here."

"Enough for lunch?" I asked, rummaging into the fruit bin beneath the far counter.

"Please."

"Where's Mrs. Hodges?"

"Out with Sally Turner for the day. You remember Sally?"

"Used to work mornings for you — married the young handyman, didn't she?"

"Hmm-hmm. She's expecting again, and Mrs. Hodges is out choosing yarns, baby linens, and what-nots. To see the two of them, you'd think it was Mrs. Hodges' own granddaughter coming."

"Are you out of sugar?"

"Shouldn't be. Try the service porch?"

"Found it—" I reappeared shortly, sugar tin

refilled. "Oh, Grandmama caught me on the way up from the beach. She said to tell you she's picking the first tomatoes."

"Good, then we can add tomato-and-onion salad to the menu." Annabel tossed a smile over her shoulder at me as I started slicing lemons. "Not too sweet."

"I can always put more sugar in mine later," I grinned.

"Your poor teeth!"

"They're sound as a horse's. Strong teeth run in my family, don't you know?"

"Not with the way you eat sweets!" she teased, hugging me about the waist as she reached 'round to dump the floury discards into the rubbish bin beneath the sink.

"So may I ask to what do we owe the pleasure of your company? I thought you had fishing tours scheduled back-to-back this week?"

"Cancellation," I grimaced. "The fellow managed to get a horrid cold, and his wife decided it was time to see a doctor. I don't think we'll be seeing them again next summer. Somehow or other the lodge gets the blame whenever someone comes down sick."

"Is it becoming a problem? In acquiring new clients or in keeping your regulars?"

"Oh no, nothing like that. It's just...," I sighed, a little discouraged. "I just hate to see unhappy patrons. I mean, this was supposed to be the poor man's vacation! Now all he's going to have to show for his time is an empty box of tissues and a few achy bones. It's not much of a holiday, I'm afraid."

Annabel smiled at me tenderly as she went to stir the soup a bit. "It's nice you care so much. A great many people would only bemoan the lost cash."

"Not if they work for Uncle Jake," I amended. "We don't put up with unreasonable demands, but we do consider it our business to 'create good memories' and not simply a summer's profit."

"So, do you have a few days off or just the afternoon?"

"Neither really. We've been so busy with excursions that some of the basic maintenance to-do's have been neglected — hence the trip down to Bemus and Maple Bay for engine parts. Paul's been coaxing life back from next to nothing for some of our smaller boats. Besides, it takes a great deal more than one canceled fare to loosen an overcrowded schedule."

"Will you be missed then? Maybe I should—?"

"Annabel," I turned about, looking at her directly, "I said I'd like to stay. They can manage without me for a time. And it'll give Paul an excuse to have himself some lunch, too."

"All right," she blushed and put the lid back on the soup pot, "you know what you're doing."

"Thank you." I bowed magnanimously, and then cheerfully added, "Anyway, it's Monday. And you always bake on Mondays."

She threw the tea towel at me.

"It's only fair for me to drop in! Not after all the trouble you go through to make me those extras loaves!"

"Only because I've noticed you have this uncanny knack for appearing when I'm baking."

I grinned, returning to my lemon assignment, and ignored the teasing gaze she tossed at me before she disappeared into the service porch. When she came back, I presented her with a glass of lemonade. Then with a contented sigh, I pulled up a counter stool to watch as she took the finished loaves from the black-and-chrome oven and slid in the next batch.

"Those scones are cool enough to go away, would you put them in the tin for me?"

"Sure.... There was something else."

"About—?"

"Why I came."

She brushed the tops of the hot loaves with butter, glancing at me expectantly.

"Paul asked me to go to the rodeo with him next Thursday, and—"

"And?"

"Well, he's got this new friend. A guy from Oregon who moved here to Gerry, to be with his grandparents or something. Anyway, his grandfather's one of the rodeo organizers and he's offering free tickets to us — the four of us, I mean. Paul was wondering if we all might like to go together? I've met his friend, Joseph Parker. He's nice, soft-spoken and — well, he's sweet."

"Sweet?" she repeated. The corners of her mouth danced slightly with some impishness.

"He really is, Annabel!"

"I'm certain he is. From what you've told me, Paul appears to attract nice, sweet gentlemen."

I didn't get her point, but she smiled quickly and amended, "Paul is a good reference, Jenny. If you both think this Joseph Parker would be a suitable escort for me, I've no objections."

"You'd like to come, then?"

She drew a deep breath and wiped her hands down the front of her apron. "That depends."

"On Grandmama?"

Annabel shook her head, drawing up another kitchen stool, and for a moment I felt an awkwardness rise between us. At seventeen, there was this older, more practical side to her than I had — or perhaps it was merely a broader sense of priorities than the routine concerns of lodge and schooling I usually dwelt upon.

"We don't—" she stopped, swallowed hard and looked down at her hands. "We still don't often talk about our family differences, Wren... or rather why there are differences."

I felt myself grow still as this most taboo of subjects surfaced for the first time since — since that awful day she'd announced their plans for Europe. But Grandmama was not here, and this did touch the two of us so very deeply, especially after last summer's absence. I gathered my courage and ventured, "You're not really referring to family class or to the social distances between old money and new, are you? You mean the other."

She didn't answer for a long time, and I raised my gaze to meet hers.

"I mean the other," she whispered.

"A much more complicated other," I amended with a sigh. "Our inexplicable time shift."

She nodded.

"Did you approach Grandmama again?"

"Yes, well...," then Annabel paused, sharing an awkward smile with me and a shrug, "at least I tried to talk with her — after we returned to the States in the fall. But when I brought up the subject...? Wren, it was one of the few occasions I've seen her get as angry with me as she does with Dickie. In the end, she presented me — or rather us — with something of an ultimatum."

"Care enough to be together or give up our summers altogether." My nod was a weary one. Grandmama Standish could be one very stubborn, old crone.

"She has her reasons for the silence, Wren." Those cinnamon brown eyes sought mine, reflecting Annabel's worries matched to my own. "All she's really asking is that we trust her."

We both shared so many of those old doubts and fears for Life's frailties. But there was the unshakable fact that we both loved Grandmama too... and I simply didn't know how not to trust her. No matter how much my reason or logic might protest, I did trust her, and I always would.

I gave another sigh and shrugged with a half-hearted grin. "So we trust her."

"Thank you." But Annabel's murmur was faint, and her pensiveness still evident as her gaze dropped.

"Do you need more?" I prompted quietly.

She hesitated, then shook her head. "No... maybe not. But sometimes it's so awkward for me, Wren."

"Awkward?" I scowled. "Being with me?"

"Not... being with you. It's more a matter of being across the lake, with you."

Listening, I waited and didn't press.

A smile fluttered across her lips, and she relaxed a bit. "It's just that some of the things you take for granted still seem frighteningly impossible to me. I — I've just assumed you never found things as difficult here on this side of the lake. At least, you've never seemed particularly put off?"

"I haven't been," I assured her. But her trepidation did make sense. "I think, it must be easier to take away things like cars and stereos rather than magically just — whoosh! Find yourself surrounded by completely foreign novelties." I paused, then I ventured, "Annabel, you needn't come to the rodeo, if you don't want to. We could always limit ourselves to the lodge — or to your own house here?"

"Oh no, Wren! I would like to go. A rodeo sounds like fun, and I've never seen a — a real cowboy." Her face brightened unexpectedly. "Do you know, nearly everyone I met in Europe wanted to know about American cowboys and Indians? They couldn't believe that I knew absolutely nothing about our 'wild west' and its harrowing cavalry battles. But me? The only Indian I know is Mr. Bannister's wife from Nantucket! And Dickie was so outraged when I dared describe a black-skinned man and his red-skinned wife as friends of our family, that — oh! It was pointless. They didn't really want to know about anyone from Rhode Island, anyway. They wanted to hear of savages fighting against industrial progress — against the civilizing power of the railroads and the struggles of new statehoods."

"Perhaps you should have told them about cars and stereos?" I teased.

"Perhaps." She nodded, a wry sort of smile rising with warmth. "Do you remember the first time I ever saw one myself?"

"One what? A car—?" With a forced laugh, I had to admit, "Yes, and for the longest time, I'd figured Paul must have done or said something awfully wicked."

"No, it was merely that strange, rusty truck-thing. Your motorboat... well, I'd become accustomed to it after those earlier summers, and it had never seemed so very odd, given I'd always known about steam engines and the paddle wheels. But it was quite a shock to watch that four-wheeled monstrosity barreling down the hill at you."

"At the rodeo, there will be a lot of those 'rusty

truck-things' — and worse."

"I know."

It took me a second or two, before I realized I wasn't understanding something. "Annabel—? Now'a'days, you don't seem to have as much problem with oddities like the trucks or such. Do you?"

"No, not so much anymore, yet...," she shook her head faintly. "Wren, one can grow somewhat immune to strange things. But the people? They expect different manners, different dress... it's difficult to blend in sometimes."

"There is an advantage to a rodeo there. Most folks are visitors... tourists. There isn't much you can do to embarrass yourself since everyone's acting a little different."

"And the money?" Her eyes met mine. "I'm well aware that my coin is unsuitable."

"Money is not an issue," I returned flatly.

"No...?" and her skepticism was plain.

I bit my lip and sighed. This was not my favorite topic. "Look, my father has always been generous with my allowance. Even if Jake never paid me a dime for my work, I'd not be hurting. The fact is, every time I ever mention money to Father, he not only writes me a check but raises my allowance substantially.

"I think it's his way of making sure I'm taken care of." But I couldn't keep the bitterness from my voice. "Between his old man's inheritance and his own product patents, he can afford to buy off his kid. He's a rich man, and by default I seem to be a rich man's daughter." I laughed at myself, "If it weren't for Jake's lodge, I'd probably never have learned anything about budgets."

Her hand closed over mine, a silent apology for bringing such harsh issues to light.

"I'm sorry," I ushered myself together. "Somehow, money seems to be the two-edged sword of my life."

She gave a small, half-laugh of self-derision and nodded vaguely as her thoughts took her elsewhere. "It plays such roles for many of us, I fear."

I looked at her, waiting.

"I never told you of Edward, did I?"

I shook my head.

"First, you should know something of my family. We have two branches... well, three now with the merchant houses open in Boston. There's the London relations and a few of their ties to the Dutch cousins and Grandmama's people in Brügg. Actually, it was almost a scandal when Grandfather married Grandmama.... You see, though she came from a good family of breeding, they were in a somewhat impoverished position. At any rate, Grandfather and his Belgium bride were promptly shuffled off to the States and the Philadelphia offices. He did surprisingly well, however, and despite the War, he even managed to expand ventures into New York City. But Grandmama always adored Philadelphia as the city of brotherly love and freedom. Its richness in all the arts, philosophies — all its traditions, she thrived there. So, Grandfather never seriously considered moving. He merely sent my father and our second cousins to oversee the growing enterprises in New York. Then after Grandfather's death, most of the Philadelphia transactions were consolidated and shifted over to New York — which is why Dickie lives in there now."

"Seems like quite a family."

"Yes," Annabel sighed in weariness. "We've become quite a family and quite a business. Now you see, it's both money and marriage which binds us all together — .from London to Amsterdam, to New York then Boston, and finally back again to London.

"There was a Maximillian emperor once—" A dry, humorless laugh escaped her. "Who once said 'Make love, not war' and then proceeded to acquire territory through a peaceful expansionism, by arranging profitable marriages for all of his children. It is a tradition, I'm afraid, which is strongly adhered to by my family.

"Heaven forbid—!" her hands flew up in disgust, "if anyone isn't interested in broadening the profits of shipping and trade! They're either disowned and left impoverished — or brought back into obedience with the threat of the disinheritance."

"Ahh," now I began to see. "Everyone was assuming then you'd marry Edward to re-consolidate the foreign and domestic ties within the family. I hadn't quite understood, why it seemed you were simply expected to stay with him."

"Well, money calls to money — or so they say," Annabel noted with sarcasm. "Grandmama has always maintained the lot of them are snobs. After having the pleasures of meeting so many of them, I'm afraid I agree with her."

"Was Edward a snob too?"

"A snob?! A sordid, egotistical, money-monger would be closer to the truth!"

Startled, I raised an eyebrow. She never described people so uncharitably!

"Don't look at me like that. It's true!"

"I don't doubt it," I assured her quietly. "I'm thinking he must be far worse for you to even say as much."

"I'm sorry." She sighed shortly, relenting. "I didn't mean to snap at you."

"It's all right. Go on."

"He's — he's just one of those people who can't think of a thing to say unless it's about himself or his business. He's patronizingly courteous to any and all ladies. But he pointedly puts a woman in the wrong — whether it be a case of fact or opinion — within a mere breath of her speaking. It doesn't matter if he's right or wrong! But, naturally, he was always certain he was right!"

"You noticed differently?"

"Wren, I might not know a lot about a lot of things, but art and especially my own paintings, are certainly not my weak points."

"Go on."

"Then there was Dickie! Maneuvering me into ballroom corners, outings in the park and — oh, anything to push me close to Edward! I felt like when we were youngsters, with Dickie showing up his smug, over-bearing egotism at everyone else's expense! It was as if he'd sent my little model ship out into deep water again, threatening — laughing at the fact that I wasn't going to be able to do a thing! I was — I was just going to lose one way or another!"

"Only you weren't there to show him differently. So I did!" Her cinnamon eyes blazed with a red fury I'd seldom, if ever seen, as she faced me full. "I stopped playing the mild, unassuming guest and retaliated."

"Grandmama Standish enjoyed that, I'll wager."

"Yes!" She actually threw back her head and laughed. "Yes, I think she did."

"So how did you do it?"

"I piped up and debated historical context whenever the men rambled on about expansionism and isolationism. I split hairs about the definitions of art and its compatibility with photography, while maintaining photographs were not about to replace the paint brush. When they professed mechanization to be largely at the height of it's glory, I reminded Dickie that his own precious Lord Salisbury—"

"Who?"

"Robert Cecil — English Prime Minister?"

"Ohh… right." Thatcher wouldn't be in office for about eighty years yet, I reminded myself.

"Dickie fairly worships Salisbury as the ideal — birthright of the gentry and all. Well, I reminded him that even Lord Salisbury had just harnessed the Hatfield River for electricity — evidence that the merit of modern machinery is only on its threshold of potentials! I succeeded in arguing myself right out of the ladies' parlors!

"It sent Dickie into furies and Grandmama into titters. But Edward," she sobered suddenly. "I'll never underestimate a man's strength again, Wren. He accosted me in the gardens at a ball one evening, fuming at my 'insensitivity' to the natural order of things."

"His definition of 'the natural order' being man's superiority over woman?"

"Yesss!" It came out with a hiss. "If Grandmama hadn't insisted Dickie come searching for me, my snobbish cousin would have precipitated a rather sordid, engagement announcement."

My fists clenched, and I had to work to keep my voice level. "Did he hurt you?"

"Only my pride. He barely kissed me—" She paused to draw a more even breath. "Dickie was adamant that I had instigated the whole, untidy affair, and — the gall of my brother! He actually apologized in my name to that cad."

"And…?"

"And I'm still engaged to the fiend! Can you believe that? Grandmama near tore Dickie's head off him, but she decided an immediate, tactical retreat was more to our advantage. So we came home. But — blast it, Wren! Sometime in the next few years this man is going to settle into the Boston offices and then appear in Philadelphia, to claim my hand in marriage. It's the most frustrating — infuriating position to be in! And all he truly wants is my father's money and the trade contracts!"

"Money again," I saw and did my best to release the internal knot of anger cramping in my stomach. "Will you marry him?"

"No," her mouth set firm. "Grandmama says I need not. She's always said life is made of choices and that I need not to marry anyone if I don't wish.

"Also...," Annabel smiled with a bit of irony, "I suspect, Edward may want to marry long before Grandmama ceases her protests. After all, there is an age where I'll become something of an irascible, old spinster, and such old maids are seldom seen as attractive catches, contracts or not."

"All of this, just because of your money."

"It's not even my own, Wren! It's Dickie's really. I'm just the bank note, so to speak."

"Not just," I corrected, smiling with mischief of my own. "It seems you're becoming rather sticky with complications. Edward may very well decide he doesn't want anything quite so troublesome."

An impish dimple sprouted, "So Grandmama suggests, too."

* * *

I waved politely to the trio in the old, cheerful blue-and-white rowboat, and as they approached I rose from the bench to help them dock. I smiled as M'dam Randolph chattered on about the evening's moon and the perfect atmospheric something-or-others. She was a charming, if slightly eccentric woman, and her niece was quieter than a mouse, as usual. I don't think I'd ever heard the young woman — in all the seances and dinners I'd attended for Grandmama — once utter a full sentence. Of course, I mused as Mr. Thomas graciously handed his passengers ashore, if I had an aunt as verbose as M'dam Randolph, then I too might value silence.

The women hurried towards the house, M'dam precariously catching the heel of a high ankled boot in the dock boards. With barely a break in either's stride, the niece calmly reached out to steady the mounds of frilly, floppy lace which comprised her aunt. While obliviously, M'dam chattered on.

There is a place over on Cassadaga Lake called Lily Dale. It's a village settled with herbalists, palmists, and fortune-tellers of various, colorful heritage. The county gossip-mongers adore prattling on about the residents' oddities and crystal balls, and often as not the joke is that circus sideshows which can't afford to retire — or merely winter — in Florida will find their way to Lily Dale. M'dam Randolph would object there, clarifying her reasons for settling there were due to cosmic what-nots. For the most part, however, the local disbelievers and the fortune-tellers generally ignored one another. Although I couldn't help but notice, a few neighbors periodically sought spiritual counsel from the star dust and moonlighters of the old Victorian township.

"Are you joining us tonight, my dear?"

"Afraid not," I turned back to Mr. Thomas with a smile.

A thin man of mid-thirty and barely my height, Mr. Thomas professed to be a lawyer by trade as well as a "dabbler" in the Tarot cards. I expect one might need a few good lawyers in a place like Lily Dale, especially if customers took displeasure in their fates...?

His fingers smoothed the brim of the white Panama hat he held, a perfect compliment to the baggy, white summer suit he wore. "It's a pity. M'dam is hoping to reach beyond the pearly gates."

I could never tell if Mr. Thomas was speaking in earnest or jest. "For Grandmama's husband?"

He nodded placidly, the wind ruffling his dark hair despite the liberal dosing of hair tonic he'd obviously given it. "Are you certain you won't stay?"

"My apologies, but there are other commitments—" and I shrugged.

"Yes, well," he sighed, donning his hat, "the young must have their adventures. We will miss you, but do have a pleasant evening."

"And you too, sir—"

He turned back unexpectedly, pulling a small card from his vest pocket. For a moment, he hesitated as his fingers toyed with the thing. Then with a slight nod of decisiveness he extended me his business card. "Grandmama Standish requested you have this, in case you have a need to — attempt contact with Annabel or Herself during the winter months. I'm not quite certain if I could be of any help to you in such a circumstance. But I naturally would do my best, to do whatever was possible."

I glanced at the Lily Dale address a bit quizzically. Something seemed out of place on that little card. It was the phone numbers, I realized with a shock; they were seven digit numbers with area codes. Mr. Thomas and company were my contemporaries — not Annabel's!

Then suddenly — glancing at the row boat moored behind my own motorboat — another piece of these summers with Annabel became clear. It was my lake. When the Standishes were in residence, this lake became the gate between Annabel's time and mine — the lake front was a far distance from the house on the hill, cloaked by the line of trees across the sloping lawn, so neither noise nor sight ever announced my motorboat's presence to guests or delivery folk. And no one other than Grandmama or Annabel had ever actually witnessed my arrival or departure... save for Dickie on that first day Annabel and I'd met, and then Uncle Jake had been in a row boat just as Mr. Thomas and M'dam Randolph always were.

Relief flooded through me like summer sunlight spills across the afternoon lake waters, joyous and believable... and the silent, dreadful isolation of my aloneness lifted. M'dam Randolph and Mr. Thomas were regular guests of Grandmama's each summer, just as Annabel and I persisted in our own meetings. If the how of it was to eternally remain some secretive — magically — inexplicable gift, it was a secret that others did share.

"Thank you, Mr. Thomas." Smiling, I was suddenly grabbing his hand and shaking it vigorously, "Thank you. You can't know how much I appreciate the thought."

"Yes... well, we shall see what we shall see. Shan't we?" He edged back, a bit overwhelmed, and I couldn't blame him as he hurried to catch up with the others.

As his flat-footed gait moved him briskly down the dock, I found my humor returning despite the shock. I never quite knew what to do with Mr. Thomas — any more than he knew what to make of me, probably. He had all the outer trappings of an experienced, polished con artist. But there was an underlying calmness in him that belied any shenanigans. In a way, I had to admit I a slight regret at missing the seance tonight. Whether I shared their beliefs or not, M'dam Randolph and company were always a lively crew to pass the time with.

Annabel's approaching figure stole my attention — and my breath. Having grown so accustomed to seeing her in long skirts and lace blouses, I almost didn't recognize her.

The mohair cowl neck of wine reds brought color to her cheeks and a rich bronze sheen to her hair. She had undone her hair knot too, weaving a French braid instead, and it made her look younger. She would never look 'just seventeen' but she no longer reflected that nebulous age of twenty-to-thirty-some either.

The dreaded blue jeans fit her not too tightly, and she'd dug out the Docksiders I'd given her earlier in the summer for her feet. Her hands burrowed deep into the pockets of her open cardigan, a blend of grey-white yarns that went well with the cowl neck. The cardigan was her favorite sweater, I knew, and tonight I suspected it was also her security blanket.

"Well?" She looked at me nervously.

"Fantastic!" I laughed and hugged her quickly. "Come on — before you change your mind."

She swallowed, chagrined at the truth in my statement. As she helped me pull the canvas from the motorboat, she murmured, "I almost went back for the skirt. When M'dam and her niece appeared, I thought — if God were kind — I would just evaporate into a little wisp of smoke and sink into the floorboards."

"You look fine," I assured her, starting the motor — still bent on getting us away before her nerve did evaporate into a little wisp of nothing. "Just look at me—!"

She did, with a rather critical eye, and for a moment I wondered myself how I fared. Pale sweater jacket, ruffled plaid cotton shirt and crisp new denims were a bit dressier than my usual attire, but nothing I was sure she hadn't glimpsed on me before.

"You're accustomed to — pants," she amended and came forward to the front seat as I set out for the lodge and rodeo. "And I like you in them."

"Life jacket!" I ordered sternly, pointing to the side rails where the flotation cushions and Mae-West jackets were stored.

She grinned, suddenly feeling on more familiar footing and pulled out the orange atrocity. "This is all a plan to motivate me into swimming lessons. Isn't it?"

I shrugged, not hiding my grin. "When I trust you can dog-paddle as far as the nearest floating cushion, I'll reconsider the vest."

She laughed and rose to one knee on the seat, turning her face into the rush of the wind. With a shout, she asked again, "There'll be real cowboys?"

"Yep — comin' in all the way from Calgary in the north and Texas from the southwest. It's an official stop on the circuit and everything!"

"Then bring on those damn'd trucks!" and she stood laughing into the rushing wind, throwing all the old qualms away for the night.

And God, she was beautiful!

Chapter Eight

That eve will always be one I remember, but not for the reasons I would have hoped. Joe and Paul were charming and fun, the evening was cool but just right for being crushed in a small mass of people, and the snow cones were as fluorescent green and ultra-sweet as ever. Annabel laughed, enjoying her first glimpse of 'real' cowboys, and Joe was flattered when we welcomed his back-stage tour. But there were moments between Paul and I which felt strained, and by the end of the evening I knew it had not been my imagination. He asked me to go for a walk after Annabel had slipped upstairs, and under the full, silver moon, he told me there was someone else in his life. That he never elaborated, that he was honest about not knowing if he even had a chance with this other — all of the details slipped by me nearly unnoticed. Amongst my own misgivings and lukewarm commitments, his reasonings didn't seem so strange. There was something missing between us, and I had beenhi a fool to think I was the only one aware of it. I had been a fool to think the decision was solely mine....

I walked back into the lodge, senses rather dulled. The night breeze had grown cold without my notice, until Uncle Jake's quiet command rang out, "Shut the door, kiddo."

With an apologetic smile, I did and wandered into the living room. It was the type of room most any lodge would host, with prize muskellunge mounted on the walls and framed maps of fishing coves scattered about. The fire was burning low now, barely more than orange embers, and Uncle Jake was in his favorite leather chair, feet propped up as he finished his latest detective novel.

"Are you waiting up for me?" I queried, leaning over the back of his chair to give him a hug.

"Maybe, maybe not. You need waitin' up for?" He pulled his glasses off of his nose and gave me a closer look, holding my arms about his neck for a moment longer.

"Hmm," he released me. "I think maybe you do tonight. "

I sighed wearily and moved around to usurp the ottoman from his feet.

"Paul?" he prodded.

I had to give him a sarcastic sort of grin, "That bad? Am I really the last to know?"

He shook his head, closing the book. "Don't know anything, sweetheart. I just guess at what I see."

"And... what do you see, Uncle Jake?"

He was quiet, but I didn't quite dare look at him. I wasn't very sure I wanted to hear his answer.

He stirred with a heavy sigh. "I see a child I care about becoming a woman, and I'm a bit lost for helping you through much of that."

His gentle gaze caught my eye then as he added, "I'm going to keep on caring about you, Jenny. Don't ever need doubt that. Hell or high water — or anything in between. It's your happiness that counts. Treat people with kindness and remember we're all a bit human with weaknesses, and then be happy. That's all that really matters, Wren. If you haven't learned that by now — between your father and myself? Well, I guess I'll just keep saying it and maybe one of these days you'll hear it, ehh?"

I nodded with a grim sort of smile. Happy was not a term my father would ever apply to himself —

useful, content — but never happy. And again I nodded "I don't want to be like him, Jake. You know that. But — sometimes, what people think about me does seem to matter, no matter how much happiness is at stake."

"True. You gotta find out who you are, and then figure the best way to live. Whether it's a quiet sort of self needing a quiet sort of path or it's a churning white waters sort of self roaring out over rapids makes no difference. You have to take — or make the way that's best for you."

"Sounds like common sense put that way." I shook my head at myself, "How come it's so hard an idea for me to hang onto?"

"Because compromises come hard sometimes. And sometimes they shouldn't be made at all. But life can be a long, long haul if you're miserable, girl.

I looked at him a little oddly, "Did you like Paul much?"

"Never had anything against him. He's a fine young fella. He's just not for you. Least, so it seemed from my vantage point." A bit of a smile peered through his bushy bread as Uncle Jake admitted, "Though it's possible, kiddo, that I'm never going to see anyone as being good enough for you. So don't go letting me tell you who to care for or who not to."

"All right. Still — can I ask what didn't seem right between Paul and me?"

Jake pursed his lips, staring hard at the fire for a long time before finally heaving a deep sigh. "You just seemed a bit too much like brother'n'sister, if you know what I mean."

"Yeah, I do know."

We let the silence hang, then Jake asked with a different note to his voice, "Any chance you could come see us for winter holidays this year?"

"Sure," I blinked in surprise at the sudden change in topics, "I'd love too."

"And the old man?"

I shrugged dismissively. "He's usually off to Boulder or San Diego for business conventions. It's the only time he's got free from the academic schedules. Frankly, I won't be missed."

"Humpf, should'a asked you a long time ago it seems. I was hopin'—" he straightened in his chair a bit, dismissing his brother. "Well then, why not for both the Thanksgiving and Christmas breaks? There's some folks, Beth's kin and friends, that I'd like you to meet. And if you're so all-fired serious about coming in with me, you should learn a little more about the winters 'round here."

"Won't Mrs. Stevens mind?"

"You're joking, ain't you?" he snorted with a laugh. "No, she won't mind. It was part her idea — a long ways back too. She thinks, you'd probably get along real fine with Jan Gregor and some others."

"Her cousin? I know Jan. She seems nice enough."

"Yep," he gave a slow, considering sort of nod, "that she is. Jan and her housemate join us every holiday. Kind of like with me... Beth and her daughter always taken in us strays. You join us, and it'll give you a chance to get to know them all better."

"I'd like that," I felt the back of my throat start to constrict with tears again. Uncle Jake always seemed to pull through when my life started tangling into knots. Damn it Paul, why couldn't you at least have waited until the end of summer?!

"You goin' be all right, Honey?"

"Been through worse, Jake." I blinked back the

watery-eye bit and swallowed hard. "I'll do fine now—"

With a gruff sort of hug, he sent me off to bed, but it didn't seem to bring a lot of comfort. The worse stuff had all had similar themes to them, I realized, swiping at the tears as I climbed the backstairs. It was a theme that Jake... and even Annabel... still followed to some extent. Everybody always went away. Jake came back, Annabel would until she couldn't... but damn it, why did Paul have to add himself to the list?

"Wren?"

I stopped just inside the bedroom door, almost startled to find Annabel curled up in the bed.

"Wren—" her voice filled with concern as she set aside her book, "what's happened?"

From somewhere, those tears which had never quite come when I left friends or Jake — when I had found Father non-existent... when I had found Mother gone — from somewhere they came now. With a sobbing choke too painful for words, I found myself falling into bed, and Annabel's arms opened to pull me near.

* * *

Winter was a revelation to me. The chilled autumn gold of Chicago turned to blasting, frigid winds. Dutifully, I hosted my father's department parties, catering his odd variety of colleagues, graduate assistants and up-and-coming undergraduates of every class... parties which brought Colleen into my life.

A freshman undeclared in her science major, Colleen proved less indecisive in her personal life, and I discovered 'chemistry' and love were not quite so far apart after all. My music began to take on much richer tones, and my children's stories went forgotten as I fumbled with more poetic verses. I began to feel those lost pieces of myself fell into place — I finally understood what Jake had been saying about compromises and happiness. Yet the decisions of secrecy and openness seemed utterly trivial when compared to the completeness I was finding within myself. It was almost as if the peace — the strength of my lake — came to make a home in my heart. It was a time to be treasured, and Colleen was a loving, bright star to delight in the treasuring.

My writing was coming into its own too, almost unbeknownst to me. Although I had near forgotten my children's stories, the dour old Professor Donavan had not. Without a word to me, Donavan sent off a few stories to a publishing friend of his, and the response was immediate and ecstatic; by Christmas I was under contract for a children's book and tentatively presenting Annabel's drawings for the illustrations. The acceptance of my work was something that both delighted and frightened me. Whether I was ready or not, adulthood it seemed had arrived.

I only wished Annabel could have been there to share the trepidation and excitement. But it was neither possible... nor part of our reality. With grim honesty, I knew I simply had to accept that, and towards the end of the holidays with Jake, I decided, I did have to face the irrevocable.

It was the last weekend of the Christmas break, nearly mid-January, and the lodge was lost in white as the snow drifted high and fell deep. The lake had finally frozen beyond its crusty edges into a solid, windblown sheet. The ice-boaters had been joyfully tacking in zig-zags since dawn, and the roar of snowmobiles drifted incessantly with the winds. The ski slopes were already open, the ice fishermen would be appearing soon, and the winter wonderland — complete with snowed in cars and snowed out offices — had definitely settled in.

At my request, Jake allowed me the use of the snowmobile for an afternoon, reminding me to be wary of damp, black patches on the ice. And I had driven the barren width of the lake to visit that lonely Victorian skeleton... all that was left from the era of the Standish summer house.

Now, as I stood knee deep in the snow, the broken down, old house looked neither yellow nor anything else. It was difficult to believe this had ever been that sunny yellow Victorian of Grandmama's delight.

It was hard in that moment to remember Mr. Thomas and his stiff, little business card with the Lily Dale address... with those modern day phone numbers, such subtle proof that come summer, this scene would change — revert into a nearly perfectly kept home. Now it was hard to see anything but the ruin of time and waste in this hollowed shell of a building.

The house, its paint wind-blasted and its structure uncared for in so many ways, no longer held any grandeur. The gingerbread trim was cracked, its jagged gaps poor outlines now of porch and eaves. The rising turrets were barely roofed, and the windows, boarded up once, now were sagging, empty abysses where the wood had split and fallen. The boathouse was barely a frame, burned out at some time or other and never rebuilt.

The wind whistled, rattling a board somewhere, and I stood with mittened hands shoved deeply into pockets, grimly feeling my world weep a little. There

had been so much love here — so much laughter, discovery — growing... and it was all reduced to nothing by such neglect. Pity rose in me, pity for those poor fools who'd had neither time nor money to see the preciousness of this house. And I regretted also that I was too late to change her — to give her back the loveliness of her summer sheen and the joy of her care-filled rooms. But she was barely a shell of a house now. The devastating damage of time — the intervening years of loss had taken their toll... and there would be no rescue by me nor by any other now.

Yet here I would stand in the tearing wind, beside this battered frame, when Annabel no longer came back. There would not be a Christmas to introduce her to Jan Gregor and Jan's woman friend. There would not be a Thanksgiving to share her bread-baking with Mrs. Stevens' family. There would never be a time to show her Chicago and the stormy, gray of that Great Lake. I would never have a winter with Annabel — . How precious summers existed was still beyond me. But I didn't care.

I merely dreaded — when there would not even be a summer.

Sometimes, when things are beyond mere logic or common sanity, it's good to pause and look closely. Not in any attempt to understand or unravel or explain the improbable, but simply in an attempt to accept... this is how it is.

Unfortunately, accepting — seeing such time-worn decay — only underlined the impossible chasm separating Annabel and I. The ache in my heart didn't ease. The ice of the winter wind seemed to bite deeper, numbing my very soul.

The Eighth Summer
Chapter Nine

They had arrived earlier then expected this year, near the end of June, and I felt my palms sweat as I brought the boat into the dock. There was so much I had to tell her this year — from Colleen to the book, and there was the all too familiar feeling of jittery excitement in the pit of my stomach that came from simply knowing I was going to see her again.

I almost worried if Annabel would recognize me, I felt so new and alive inside. Outwardly the only real change had been my hair which was cut even shorter. It was easily kept neat now; a feat I'd almost never considered to be even a remote possibility. And though I had found it agreed with my eternal tomboy-ish attitude towards life, I didn't know if she'd approve.

But of course she would approve. She had to... she was Annabel. So I donned my best denims, both jacket and jeans, and set out across the lake for an afternoon visit.

They had business attending when I appeared. The ice man, Mr. Caprino, was delivering their summer stock of ice blocks — or at least, he was trying to. Mostly, he was arguing with a young man of twenty-some years over some problem of unloading. Annabel stood to the side, hands on hips, looking absolutely adorable in her gingham dress despite a perturbed scowl. And I snuck up behind to grab her lightly around the waist.

"Wren—?!" she gasped in quiet tones, leaning back into me and briefly hugging my arms about her, and then laughed, turning within the embrace, "So early?"

"I saw your lights last night," I returned in the same hushed voice.

"I was hoping you would."

"What's their problem?" I pointed to the black boxed wagon where the two men stood, waving at a sorely chipped ice block that was half in-half out of the freezer's door.

"The wretched thing's jammed into the door lip and melting to boot. If Dickie would just let the poor man do his job—!"

So this was Dickie? I should have guessed. His bangs were still too long and still falling into his eyes, although he had outgrown the causal sweaters. His white shirt sleeves were rolled high, his silver-backed vest bulged at the side seams as he strained again to pull the icy victim free. His white linen pants were beginning to lose their crease, and his temper wasn't in much better shape. He certainly made a comical figure, and I found myself chuckling under my breath.

"Could you help?" Annabel asked suddenly, eyeing me with all seriousness.

"If they'd get out of the way, sure."

"You know...," a little bit of mischief lit in the depths of those cinnamon brown eyes, "If you tried, they'd be so flabbergasted that neither would stand in your way."

Our gazes locked. It was a tempting piece of conspiracy... and a challenge had been uttered.

"All right." I pulled the grease-stained work gloves from my back pocket, thankful for the weight of the denim jacket because I knew that ice was going to be very cold. I gave Annabel one last, inquiring look. She nodded me on ahead. I settled into my most business-like manner, striding forward to greet the men with a courteous nod.

If Mr. Caprino remembered me from previous years, he didn't show it, but then he was pretty preoccupied with Dickie. In fact, he barely noticed me as he moved aside to let me pass. He simply resettled his cap a bit, and spat at the ground — resuming an irate glaring at Dickie. As for Annabel's brother... he did the most classic double-take I've ever seen as I shouldered my way past him to confiscate both the ice pincers and his place at the door of the ice cart.

The ice chunk was too heavy to just pull over the freezer lip. It needed to be bumped up out of its chipped groove and then pulled forward by the iron hook pincers. It wasn't so different from hauling out the larger hay bails when they caught on the hinges of a pick-up truck, I thought, shouldering the icy bulk. The thing was a bit slipperier, but at least the ice wasn't going to make me sneeze like the hay did when we spread it 'cross the barn floor to soak up the motor oil.

"Mr. Caprino—?" I heard Annabel's voice claim the older man's attention, "why don't you come in for some lemonade while we leave them to the uncarting? It's freshly squeezed, and I'm sure you'll find it to your liking...?"

Thanks, I thought. Go and leave me alone with big brother.

"Just what in blazes do you—?!"

I tossed him a dour glance as I emerged from the root cellar again.

"Oh Dickie?" Annabel paused and turned briefly to lean over the porch railing, Mr. Caprino already indoors. "I don't know if you remember Wren. Jennifer Cassel? You've heard me talk of her often, I'm sure. Wren—" she graced me with the most polite and innocent looking expression I have ever seen, "my brother, Richard."

"Hello," I nodded and tugged on my glove a bit. I walked by to seize another block with the pincers. "How many of these are yours?"

I was fully into the root cellar again before I heard a flustered, "All of them!"

It was a strange hour of unloading.

* * *

"Are you terribly angry at me for abandoning you with Dickie out there?"

I had to chuckle, "Not really."

"You know, Mr. Caprino was quite impressed with your no-nonsense attitude towards my brother — but he didn't recognize you! After all those summers we pestered his poor mare, and he didn't know you."

"Well... I don't have pigtails anymore."

"I don't mind," she smiled, then went on to explain, "Apparently, he assumed you were a young man we'd brought with us from the Philadelphia household."

"And Dickie didn't dissuade him?"

"What? And have to admit a woman — his little sister's best friend, no less! — could outdo him? Not likely in the least, Wren. Of course, he didn't say anything."

"You know, I have the hardest time believing he's your brother."

"Well," Annabel smiled, picking up her skirt to step around a piece of driftwood, "you do need to remember that he was nearly ten when Grandmama took us. She says, he adopted his young-man-of-the-house manner as soon as he arrived. Grandfather was already gone, you see."

"So what's happened to all his business concerns in New York City?"

"They're calling urgently, thank heavens! Dickie's only here to see us settled in for the summer. He takes the train back week's end."

"That's still another two days. You have my condolences."

"Ohhh...." She groaned, gazing upwards. "I am sorry. He wasn't too much of a bore, was he?"

"Well, you know me. I love showing off just a little," and I grinned quite unabashed.

It was such a beautiful afternoon for a walk on the beach. There were white cotton clouds above and lazy blue waters below, and our shoes made the most satisfying clack against the stones. I felt inexplicably happy just to be here with Annabel. And none of Dickie's antics could change that today.

"You look about ready to burst," Annabel murmured and pressed, "Tell me everything, Wren. School? Plans — Jake?"

"Jake's fine," I assured her. "He and Mrs. Stevens send their regards. School's — well, I did graduate last month—"

"Who won the argument on university? You or your father?"

"We struck a compromise. Yes, I was accepted and yes I'm going, but only for the year. If I haven't changed my mind come spring, I'll transfer out here and finish up a two year program at Fredonia. And the only reason I agreed to that was because of Professor Donavan. Annabel—" I took a deep breath, "do you remember my talking about Donavan? He's in the English department—?"

"Yes. He works with you on your writing. I remember."

"Well, he sent some of the stories about Quill to a friend of his at this publishing company, and well — come Christmas this year we're going to have a book out."

"A book? Wren?" She grabbed my hands, pulling me about. "Your very own—?!"

"Our very own," I corrected, beaming. "I sent them your drawings, and they loved them."

"My sketches?"

I nodded, "And some of the watercolors. I — I wrote Mr. Thomas, your grandmother's lawyer about it. He didn't tell you?"

"Not yet, but we did just arrive."

"Yeah...," I gladly skirted that topic quickly. "Well, I wrote to ask him about contacting you to get permission to use your artwork for the book. And he said, he could handle things all right... that he has a General Power of Attorney for your affairs. So he signed for you, sent the notarized paperwork and — well?"

"Oh, he does have the right to sign for me — and for Grandmama," Annabel assured me quickly. "As a matter of fact, he's handled quite a few things here for Grandmama over the years."

"So, you don't mind. Or do you?"

"That you've—? No, I don't, Silly. I gave those pictures to you. You can do whatever you—?" she stuttered to a halt, looking completely stunned as the implications of it all finally struck, and I laughed, hugging her quick. "My pictures...? Quill's to be published?! With my...? Wren, why ever would you—?"

"You're the silly one," I coaxed, starting us up the beach again with an arm through hers. "How could I possible dream of telling our story about our Quill without your drawings?"

She shook her head, squeezing my arm. "Wren, it was your stories which interested them in the first place. Of course you can change the drawings!"

"Ut-uhh," I was firm. "And now that they've seen them, they're saying the same thing. They've asked me for a second book and want to know if you'd do at least the layouts? They'd prefer full illustrations, but my editor says she'll take what she can get. Just say the word, and they'll send all those little, nitty-gritty details about mat and color specifications."

"Wren! I don't know anything about those sorts of—?"

"We'll learn together," I interrupted. "Or they'll take what they can get, like they said they would."

"Oh, yes then, Jenny. I'd like to try, at least."

I put an arm around her waist, reminding her, "You've already got the first edition illustrated. There's nothing frightening in 'trying' anything now. They love your work."

"They love *our* work," she amended warmly. "And thank you, Wren. You couldn't have given me a more wonderful present."

We drifted a few steps apart then as we walked on. I bent to pick up a flat stone, feeling my mouth grow dry as I held onto my next piece of news. It was an awkward, confusing excitement that was making me tongue-tied.

"There's more, isn't there?" Annabel noticed shortly. "About the book — about school?"

I laughed nervously, "Not quite."

"The lodge?"

"No," I swallowed, shaking my head, and I sent the stone skipping out over the water.

She eyed me sideways, a particularly bland expression falling across her face with, "A man?"

"No," I gulped, "a woman."

Bravely, I chanced to meet her glance. "Her name is Colleen Hansen. She's about a year older than I am, and... and... "

"You love her," Annabel finished quietly.

"Yes."

The silence hung between us for a while. Then in a moment, I began to panic. I was wrong. She had lied to me last summer! This was going to make her hate me.

"Last — last year, on our first night back together, you mentioned some of the women who gathered among Grandmama's parlor guests...? You said, it wouldn't make a difference? That it was—"

"Of course it makes a difference!" Swiftly she rounded on me, concern reflected in her eyes. "Just look at yourself Jenny, you're happy. I've never seen you so happy, at least not since I've returned from Europe." Annabel slipped her arm through mine, pressing me close, "It makes a wonderful difference, and I'm happy for you. I am. Now tell me about her. Colleen is it? Where did you meet? What's she like?"

It felt strange talking to Annabel, describing another who seemed so much a part of my foggy half-life in Chicago. As I said the words, I found myself less and less aware of my feelings for Colleen and more attuned to the woman beside me... attuned to where all that nervous excitement had always come from. Colleen's hair was almost the same shade as Annabel's, when Annabel had been younger — but there was more gold here now. Colleen's blue eyes had always startled me whenever I looked at her. Today I saw why... they should have been that certain shade of brown — that cinnamon spice hue of red-brown. Colleen should have been a little less tall... her air a little less hurried.

She should have been Annabel.

"Then you'll be with her at the university come fall?"

"What?" I blinked, disconcerted and feeling at a loss.

"Will you be seeing her in the fall?"

I swallowed and nodded vaguely. Seeing her, yes... but I suddenly knew, Colleen and I weren't going to make it through the summer. Like the brilliant evening star she was, Colleen had passed through my life making dreams come true. But she was the stuff dreams were made of — not everyday life... at least, not my life.

Then I wondered, if I could be content with just summers.

The image of that desolate house set in winter white returned to me. And I realized the question rather was — how would I manage without even the summers?

Chapter Ten

D o you think it would work?" Annabel asked, tentative even in her excitement.

We were standing in the Keeper's room of the old boathouse. The men had finished painting the outside earlier in the week. They were busy now with the porch and trim on the main house, and so the room was still littered with their supplies and rags. It was also crowded with rusty odds'n'ends from the garden and with a dilapidated sailboat. Behind the clutter, though, there was a reasonably good-sized room. The windows were intact, if grimy, and the small fire hearth in the end wall of stone didn't seem to be crumbling.

I chewed on my lips, frowning some. Surprisingly, the place didn't smell very dank despite the rough, unfinished wooden walls, and the bare rafters above. Those beams were coated with almost as much dirt as the floorboards. Experimentally, I stomped on the floor a bit.

"The boards seem sound," I admitted, almost muttering to myself. At least they felt pretty solid under my feet, and the wall panels weren't warped. I sighed, hands on my hips as I turned back to Annabel. "You're sure the painters would clear this junk out and sand everything down before painting?"

"They even suggested it themselves, Wren. But I don't want to waste the time nor money if—?" She ended lamely with a shrug.

"Well, I don't see why not try," I grinned, taking pity on her hopeful pensiveness. "It ought to do just fine as long as they'll do the basics. I'd offer myself, but I just don't know when I'd get the time together to—"

"Oh no! I don't want you to do anything like that." Then she smiled, arms wrapped about herself — nearly hugging herself to death to contain her glee. "I was so wishing, Wren! I want it so much that I was afraid I wasn't being very practical."

"No," I rejoined her in the doorway and squeezed her shoulders in reassurance, "you're not seeing things. It does look like a good place for a studio."

"I have an attic room at home — in Philadelphia, I mean. With a marvelous skylight. But here I always seem to be interrupted by one thing or another. And with all the trees around the house there's so little light—"

"With all the cloud cover above, don't you mean," I corrected, amused.

"Wren!" she jabbed me with her elbow.

"All right!" I pushed my hands into my back pockets, politely putting on my best behavior. "I'll be serious...."

* * *

It was her show of independence, that studio room. New rules developed for the household. Daily help and Mrs. Hodges accepted the boathouse as off-limits, and even Grandmama respected Annabel's newly proclaimed need for privacy and painting. She blossomed beyond the poised young woman I had always known her to be, and she gained a self-confidence that went much deeper than outward appearances. Somewhere, in the corner of my mind — as I watched her paintings mature into polished illustrations, as I watched her landscapes develop from pretty pictures to personal perceptions — I realized that the helpless feeling I'd once fought against when she'd turn, looking for answers had not just been my own anxiety. It had been as much a part of her fears of being a girl with so little say in her life — as it had been my inner fears of inadequacy. Yet now, the doubts were receding in her even as Dickie's letters ranted on about marriage and family responsibilities; that summer marked her Coming of Age much more than any society debut could ever have. And I felt incredibly proud to find she included me in the process... the boathouse was never off limits to her lakeside friend.

But as with all our summers, we were haunted with realities too — and that year spawned a subtle pain I don't think either of us will ever forget.

"Well hello there," I glanced up as her shadow drew my attention away from my music. "You look quite pleased with yourself. What happened in class?"

Annabel's smile broke into a pleased, very girlish giggle as she sat herself down on the park bench with me. Her art supplies and portfolio set safely down on the ground beside her. "Andy thinks these are marvelous! He says there's no reason in the world why your editor should turn them down!"

"All right! Success!" I strummed her a chord from the guitar in my lap. "Sweet success!"

"And—"

I waited expectantly, eyebrows raised.

"He's asked that I come back next week — for the advanced series."

"This is good?" I asked, feeling like I was missing something.

She nodded emphatically. "Invitational only —

special projects and lots of individual attention. I think I've just made the professional tiers!"

My smile was delight enough and she grabbed me and hugged me, guitar and all.

I thought my heart was going to stop dead.

"I told him I wasn't certain if I would accept. But Wren! The honor at being asked!"

I swallowed as she released me and dragged my mind back into reality. "So, do you want to study an extra week or so with this man? It's up to you. My music tutorials go all summer, and I do have a little flexibility in rescheduling them since they're private lessons. We could work something out to get you here."

"Oh, I don't know," she sighed, almost pouting for an instant. Then, "I'm just so excited at — at knowing I am good. I mean, there isn't anybody in my family who really understands much about this sort of painting, you know? I miss not having — I mean you're the only one who even knows what I'm actually doing! To everyone else they're just nice little pictures. And acknowledgment feels so good! I get so — so dependent on your comments that sometimes it feels like I'm abusing you, and I don't want that. And when we disagree, I can't always tell if it's just our opinions clashing or if it's the content failing."

"I know what you mean." I grinned, ironically knowing it only too well. "Uncle Jake is quite nice about my stories and would be mortally offended if he thought he was being unsupportive in any way, shape or form. But he's not a writer any more than Grandmama is a painter... any more than I'm a painter, actually."

Her smile turned warm and soft, and she placed a gentle hand over my fingers as they toyed with the guitar keys. "You don't have to be a painter to understand what's important to me, Wren. You truly don't. It's something I can share with you. You listen and understand what's difficult when there's a problem, you remember what's subtly different in styles and perspectives after I've shown you, and you care enough to always be asking about my work. You know more about what's important to the painter in me than some of these instructors do."

"Probably just the leftovers from traveling with Mother."

"Probably...," but she was smiling like I was an adorable, wet porcupine, and that made it okay.

"So," I switched directions, partly to get my heart beating again, "does this mean you want to take classes next week or not?"

She shook her head a bit absently. "He doesn't need an answer until Friday...."

"Is there a reason not to take his class?"

"Not a reason — I just don't know if they'd actually do me any good at this point. In another year, maybe, but now?" She glanced at me, "Can I let you know end of this week? Or will planning so late make problems with your lodge schedule?"

"No," I assured her, "Jake and I have a very quiet week next week. Everyone coming in is a regular, and they seldom want guides. Friday will leave me more than enough time to sort through things."

She relaxed with a contented sigh. Then smiled as she looked around the park, the wind blowing loose strands of hair into her eyes. "I think Grandmama might just like this place here in your time-and-day."

I glanced around, noticing the square for the first time in a while. I was so familiar with Chautauqua that it was rather a thing I took for granted. But it was a nice town square, with the stone fish at the fountain gurgling happily and with the massive oaks and maples shading the crosswalks. It was a peaceful and lazy atmosphere where the red brick walls and stately white columns of the post office and administration-shopping buildings blended time smoothly back to the older buildings beyond the square, to the boarding houses and summer cottages (some of which did date back to before the turn of the century). But Chautauqua had neither a stale nor stodgy "old" feeling to it these days. True, prohibition might still be in vogue here, but the musical and fine arts influences now grossly outweighed the soap-box preachers, and the stately hotels probably hosted more Jewish widows than Protestant reformers these days. The modern art museum, a rough dark shingled little cottage from the outside, was a forerunner of hideous monstrosities, and the amphitheater was just as apt to host Burl Ives or Tanya Tucker as it was to sponsor the Cincinnati Ballet, although the weekly symphonies were still always filled. It had come a very long way from the days when the administration had cancelled Susan B. Anthony's speaking engagement (actually, she'd ended up in Lily Dale and half the Chautauqua guests had journeyed over to hear her anyway). Still, the place was probably the oddest mixture known to any summer fine arts institute, and so unique enough to have survived in one form or another since the days of the paddle-wheels.

"Do you know," Annabel mused, waving at a tattered jeaned and T-shirted pair from her art class as they crossed the far side of the park, "Grandmama tells of the most narrow-minded, unbending cads that inhabit this place. "

"Well, there was a time when they refused to let

a boat land simply because it was Sunday."

She grinned with a bit of mischief, "Must be Dickie's doing."

I laughed at that.

"What do you think they're up to over there?" she nodded at the exhibition boards which were being set into place down near the Pavilion.

"A *Turn of the Century Photo Essay*," I quoted in my most officious voice.

She laughed. "You got let out early today, didn't you?"

"Well... yes," chagrined, I admitted it. Whenever I got out of class early, I rarely spent the extra time practicing — I usually walked through the museum or browsed through the bookstore, which meant I often picked up the special event bulletins.

"Well, it's not like I'm going to do anything professional with my music." I unsnapped the capo from my guitar's neck, taking an inordinate amount of interest in doing it.

"It's practically your life, Wren!" But she was smiling at me.

"No, the lodge is my life."

"The lodge is your home and your income."

I shrugged, "My writing is what's important."

"Yes, and so your music has lyrics."

"It's just a hobby!"

She almost choked on that one.

"It is."

"A very obsessive hobby, wouldn't you say?"

I found myself blushing and stowed the guitar in its case with as much speed as I could manage.

She squeezed my elbow reassuringly, then nodded towards the exhibit. "Do we have time to look?"

"If you like, they ought open up in about an hour."

There was a wistful air about her, and I took pity on our mutual plight. "How about lunch first?"

It was her turn to blush. "Transparent am I?"

"Like glass."

"Can we put my portfolio in the boat first?"

"Along with my guitar. I'm sick of lugging it around today."

"It is rather auspicious—!"

"Careful—"

"I have the hardest time believing people actually wear those things," Annabel whispered. Her ice cream cone discretely pointed down the exhibition aisle to a young woman dressed in cut off denims and a bathing suit.

I hid my smile, murmuring, "Soft Serve Ice Cream and Skin Tight Swim Wear — all comes with the territory, Darlin'."

"One has absolutely nothing to do with the other!" she hissed, and I noticed she was actually blushing.

"What's wrong with it?" I challenged with a more serious curiosity. "She's covered."

Annabel tipped her head, amused as she looked at me, and waved her napkin surreptitiously down her front. "Don't you find an itty-bitty bit of a contrast here, Jenny?"

As usual, she was plainly dressed in blouse and long skirt. The top wasn't quite as lace adorned as she might have worn around the lodge or at Grandmama's, but the thin brocade trim on the dark skirt made it less austere in spite of its cut. It was a comfortable compromise between her naturally more formal style and the lazy casualness of many around us. It was actually not so odd here at the Institute where many of the widows still wore black lengths long after their husbands' deaths and where artists or students were often dressed for some dramatic effect. Actually, her clothes wouldn't have been too terribly out of place anywhere in the county. True, it was more pristine than the over-worn blue jeans, but in an area where Mennonite and Amish families were known and where the Golden Age of Homespun was still celebrated every summer with quilt auctions and Blue Grass music barbecue', her style of dress was almost more acceptable than many of the current fashion fades from the cities.

"But you've never minded me in a one piece? And she even has shorts on."

Her flush deepened. She turned primly to stare at the photograph in front of us, and she ate her ice cream.

"Or have you been uncomfortable and not telling me?" I suddenly found that to be an outright insulting thought.

"You're — different."

"Why? Do I have so many freckles that I don't need a blouse?" I teased. Then, lowering my voice I added wickedly, "Don't tell me you're becoming a prude?!"

"Not likely," she giggled and moved us on to the next row of pictures.

We walked about in silence for a few more minutes, my attention span plainly wandering as I crunched my way down to the bottom of my cone. After so many hours of watching people paint (and especially Annabel), I was discovering I didn't much care for black-and-white photos.

"You know, it just may rain on them tomorrow," I glanced up rather philosophically through the leafy branches. "I wonder what they do with all this stuff, when a real downpour hits?"

"Swarm around like busy bees, bundling everything inside, I should imagine," Annabel returned, her dimple showing. But she paused in her study of a photo to look overhead. "Will it be bad enough that we shouldn't risk coming tomorrow?"

"Don't think so. Forecast is merely for cloudy. Shouldn't actually rain, although around here you never can tell."

She tossed me a teasing look, "And sometimes you can, Jennifer Cassel, but choose to let insanity rule instead."

"Me?" I was shocked. "When I have ever taken anybody out boating when it wasn't safe?"

"You took yourself," she reminded me. "Last year, when you came over on the first night."

"Oh—" I swallowed hard. "That wasn't foolish. That was just impulsive. Foolish would have been going home in the lightning."

"Which you were planning to do."

"Planning doesn't count," I muttered. "Besides, that wasn't just any, old storm. We near set records for July rainfall last year. Probably hasn't been anything so wicked since — since—"

"—Since 1897?" Annabel offered impishly.

With something of a half-grin, I managed a shrug. The reminder of our differences was a little more painful when it got so concrete. But as Annabel had moved on to the next isle of photos, I determinedly pushed aside the melancholy. Hurrying after her, I found myself abruptly halting as I almost ran into her on the other side of the display wall.

"I know her—" Annabel stood there utterly motionless, staring quite intently at the photograph before her.

"What?"

"I know her...," but Annabel's voice was fading, and she had paled with shock.

I turned to look at the picture. It was a self-portrait of the photographer Käsebeir, a woman perhaps in her thirties. It was an interesting play with light and shadows, but there was nothing particularly striking to my inexperienced eye.

I placed a steadying hand to Annabel's elbow, worried by the stillness in her. Then suddenly she moved, turning to glance quickly at the pictures all around her with a haunted panic.

"Annabel, what is it?"

She licked her lips nervously, her fingers clutching my arm, "I — I don't think I should be here."

"Why—? Sure, okay. Come on," and I snatched the ice cream cone from her trembling fingers before it fell, dropping it in the trash as I pulled her away from the open air show. There were times I knew better than to demand explanations, and this was definitely one of them.

A shadowy coolness swallowed us, adding distance between us and the exhibition. I glanced at her warily and ventured, "Are you all right now?"

She just shook her head and walked faster.

Beyond the amphitheater, down the lane towards the lake there is a small gorge with benches beside it and yawning trees hiding the sky above. It is a place that sometimes feels icy and chilled even when the stoic houses on either side are bathed in yellow sunlight. But it's a place that offers respite from hustle and notice, and it was a place of privacy that I welcomed now.

"Sit," I ordered, and she did, nearly collapsing onto the bench with a hand to her stomach and her breath coming in short pants. I had one horrid moment when I feared she was about to pass out on me, and silently I cursed the corset I knew she was wearing.

"Easy now," I put a hand against the nape of her neck, gently massaging the tight muscles, and she sat back, leaning into my touch... drawing a steadier breath. "Just take it easy."

She gave a grateful gasp and sent me a rather self-humored little glance. "Sorry—"

"It's all right," I allowed. "Take your time."

"Has anyone ever told you—?" she paused with her eyes half-closed, forcing a deeper breath, before "Have they ever told you, you'd be a good mother?"

"Not really," I laughed, letting her move away from me as she sat up a bit more.

"Patience — first thing needed."

"Then we'd both be good moms," I amended, still not pushing her. She was going to tell me in her own time.

Her one hand unconsciously reached for the locket hung around her neck. Gently, I took the other, realizing she was strongly needing to feel connected.

"I'm just being silly," she murmured then, staring off into that shady little gorge.

"You said you knew her — Käsebier?"

Annabel nodded slightly, her clasp tightening in mine.

"That's certainly not unusual." I scowled. "She's a well-known photographer. She was a wife — mother... a feminist renowned for attempting to catch the spirit of a woman with her lens. Why shouldn't you know her? Even I know her."

"No," Annabel returned firmly, "I know her."

I looked at her blankly.

"I've met her."

My teeth caught the inside of my lip as understanding came. Sometimes I'm amazed at how slow my wits turn.

"In Grandmama's parlor. But — Wren, she's dead now."

"Oh boy...," I felt my own breath grow long and slow. This was not one of those "little" details of difference. This was a significant one. How could I have not anticipated something this potentially disturbing for her?!!

"It's just—" Annabel gestured weakly at nothing in particular. "I shouldn't have been there, Wren. She's — she's not particularly anything special, not the photographer I know. I don't even know her very well! I paint little animals — cute and cuddly. She does poetic statements with photo portraits — shadows and light.... We've not much in common, I suppose. And she's not around very often. She's more a friend-of-a-friend. Bu-but she's not—!

"Don't you see, Jenny? I wouldn't have ever thought twice about her work. But now — Wren, she's someone! How — how do I go back and just pretend that I don't — that she's not going to develop into this!!

"That I even go back at all...?" She bit her knuckle, her face draining white again. "Dear heavens — what is she doing to us...?"

I pulled myself together. She was going to fade on me if I didn't. "Who, Annabel? Who's doing what to us?"

She bowed her head into her hand, "Grandmama — I think."

"Grandmama loves you, Annabel," I began softly. "She'd never want to hurt you."

"But she does anyway, Wren," she shook her head aimlessly, and I realized she was crying. "She does so much—"

I felt way out of my depth as that wicked, bittersweet helpless feeling surfaced again.

"I'm sorry—" and as suddenly as it began Annabel seemed to be recovering. With a sniffle she sat straighter, searching her pockets for a handkerchief. "I am being foolish. You're right, naturally. We've always known Time and things were different for us. It's foolishness to complain now."

She forced a laugh, sparing me a glance, "It's been how many years—?"

"Since we were eleven."

"And I choose now to be upset? But then," she took a gentler hand to herself, "how often do I see the face of someone I know...? Someone looking so much older than how I know her to be... until I realize that here and now, she's already been dead for...."

I slid back into the bench seat, turning to gaze into those nebulous shadows of the gorge. Then pensively, "Do you know how Grandmama does it?"

Annabel shook her head. "In all honesty, I'm not certain she's doing all of it."

I didn't quite glance at her. "Are you helping her?"

She paused to think, then reluctantly shook her head. "Not that I know of. I should think I'd know — wouldn't I? If it were of my own doing?"

"I'd think so." I studied my hands. I felt them tremble, although outwardly they seemed quite steady.

"I know Mrs. Hodges certainly isn't."

"True," I murmured in agreement. "Only

Grandmama's ever warned you about trusting yourself, when things seem strange."

"Or rather she used to... she doesn't so often anymore."

"You're much older now."

"I'm much more frightened now."

I looked at her with that. She suddenly seemed very little and very scared. "What can I do to make it less frightening, Annabel?"

The softness of her mouth trembled, then stiffened with her pain. Her eyes grew wide and blinked quickly at burning tears. And I took her hands in mine, finding them cold and stiff. "What can I do?"

Her head shook vaguely, and her voice was hoarse with effort, "Not go away—"

"I won't!" I pulled her near, with her head to my shoulder, and I held her tight, rocking us both so gently. "I promise, Annabel. I won't go."

Yet it was a liar's vow. Because of course, come summer's end... I would.

The Ninth Summer
Chapter Eleven

The sunlight streamed through the studio window washing over her with a warm caress — catching the gold and that hint of autumn bronze which gleamed in her hair.

My fingers faltered, the rhythm lost, and for a moment I shut my eyes against her beauty, forgetting my guitar. But it did no good; I could still see her even behind closed lids as she bent at her desk, intent on the fine ink details she sketched into the colors on her rice paper.

With a sigh, I turned to the music beside me. Vivaldi needed more concentration than I could muster together today. Absently, I began to massage my aching fingers. I wondered if there was anything I could manage today? My gaze drifted to the chaise I sat upon, and my mouth dried as I realized there was indeed something I could have managed quite well.

The chaise was actually a small brass bed, with an odd assortment of pillows scattered along the wall for backing. I was not thinking of it as a place to sit.

My fingers flexed and I stared, slowly turning my hand. Years of strumming and picking had made them strong hands... graceful hands, with no trace of sandpapery skin or scars from fishing tackle, although my left hand did have the habitual calluses of the guitar player. But perhaps those practiced years of precision playing had made me less apt to slip with bait and hook or less prone to careless snips by pliers? Or maybe, it was simply my lack of mechanical puttering. I rarely took a hand with motor repairs, and balancing the accounts was not so hard on one's skin.

I felt the heat rise through my face and my insides melt to sweet wetness. I remembered, there was another sort of music these hands had mastered.

My palms tingled with a softness only imagined. I scowled at myself, rubbing the feeling away quickly. Annabel was my friend, and somehow it seemed disloyal to allow such fantasies to surface. She had never given me any reason to think along those lines.

"Are your hands hurting again?"

Annabel's quiet murmur drifted to me, and guiltily I jumped. But she had not looked up from her work. I grinned at myself. I had it pretty bad. A little sunlight and her back to me and here I was chastising myself for these nebulous fantasies of her. To borrow a quote from my friend there — Lord love a duck!

She turned then, my silence drawing her around. "Wren?"

"No, I'm fine," I denied quickly, shaking my hand to loosen the muscles. "I'm just not concentrating very well."

"Anything in particular?"

"Not in the least," I asserted smoothly. Cheerfully, my fingers took up another tune.

"Lazy days of misty raindrops—"

She smiled as my voice half-faltered, and I found being flippant had been dangerous after all. I had never meant for her to hear this song!

"Pull my cloak away to find my soul—
so fine — a touch—"

But I knew better than to stop and give myself away.

"And the day is warmed by our song—
the love is bright within your laughter.
My heart is won, by your quiet ways—
as your gentle kiss ensnares my mind—
so fine—"

I felt my face grow sheepishly red and thanked the stars the lyrics were rather innocent.

"Let time drift by with our tenderness—
as the rain plays on — across the rooftops—"

And thank God it was short too!

"—pull my cloak away to find my soul—
so fine — a touch — so fine — a touch—"

I finished with my usual flourish and gave her a shrug as I glanced up, planning to bluff my way through with nonchalance.

But the delight in her face had faded and her smile seemed vacant. Her words came only slowly after what seemed to be an eternity of silence, "I haven't heard that one. Did you write it for Colleen last year?"

"Last year, but... well, not particularly—"

If my vagueness registered, I don't know, as she was already turning to reach for her pen again. But I welcomed her distraction, hiding myself behind another piece of music. The last thing I had ever wanted to do was make her feel uncomfortable; unfortunately, it seemed I had failed.

* * *

I sat up a straighter as my line tugged — just a little. Again, that beguiling twitch of a nibble came, and I caught my lower lip between my teeth. This one was too crafty for a hit-and-run; if he was lucky he'd eat around the hook and leave me with nothing. But if I timed it just so—.

Jake was still, watching me out of the corner of his eye. He hadn't missed my sudden tension.

The pull barely started again — I jerked hard.

"Got'm!" but he wasn't landed yet.

The rod bent as the fish fought the line in the depths below. My breath stopped as I reeled and sought to keep the tension steady in the pull. There was no telling how well the hook had or hadn't set. He was far from being caught.

"Easy...," Jake's encouragement was barely a murmur, but there was excitement in his voice, too.

The rod bounced as the fish reversed to an upward direction. But I stayed with him and the hook didn't shake.

"Crafty critter," Jake was grinning now. "Must be a big one."

With a sudden lift, the fish flew clear of the water, flipping white — silver flashing as it struggled in mid-air. But the hook was well set and he danced, slowing until he was worn out. Then the bass merely waited, dangling.

"What a beauty!" Jake laughed, reaching for the line as I brought it nearer.

The thing began another round of flip-flopping, but Jake was skilled and sure as he took the fish in hand to work the hook free from its mouth. The white bass was a gorgeous size, nearly fourteen inches and plump; quickly Jake slipped the stringer through its mouth and gill before dropping it overboard with the rest of our catch.

"We'll going to eat well tonight," Jake applauded, rinsing the scales from his hand in the lake water.

"Some should go in the freezer," I pointed out rather practically. "I don't expect us to eat half a dozen each."

He chuckled, "You're assuming our guests haven't been unlucky."

"Jake, they're old pros. They'd be insulted if they weren't eating their own catch, and you know it."

"Never hurts to have a few on hand, just in case."

"Have you looked in the freezer lately?"

"Breaded, broiled or stewed," he shrugged, passing me a minnow from the bait bucket, "it all saves money on the groceries come winter."

"That's beginning to sound like a threat," I teased, but he just shook his head and laughed.

We settled back down, the wind cool as it cut through the sunlight of late afternoon. And I thought it was a good feeling to be spending time with Jake out here, knowing I wasn't going to be parceled off to Chicago this fall. It was an uncommonly good feeling for a plain routine.

"What's got you grinning?"

"Nothing much." I turned my smile on him. "Was just thinking how glad I am to be here." I chided myself a little, "You'd think after seventeen years of smelly fish, dank seaweed, and incessant cloud-cover I'd have gotten it out of my system."

He nodded, an understanding completely. "Some things we never do get enough of."

"Yeah... have I told you thanks yet?"

His bushy brows lifted in mute question.

"For takin' me in."

"Buying in, you mean?"

"That too," I amended.

"Well," he rubbed his thick, ruddy beard a bit, "you're not partnered yet, kiddo."

"Still doubting me?" I tossed back. We both knew the contracts and bank notes were only going to be formalities come the end of next summer.

"Not doubting, Honey," Jake chuckled. "More just disbelief. It's hard for me sometimes to remember you're my brother's daughter."

"In most ways, I'm not." I shook my head, amazed to discover most of the bitterness was finally gone.

He seemed almost shy, "Seems more like you're my own."

Touched, I returned his gaze warmly. "As I said, thank you for taking me in."

Our attention wandered back to the fishing lines, the billowy clouds still drifting lazily above. It was a good sort of day.

"I've been keeping you pretty busy this summer, haven't I?"

"Not particularly." I glanced at him in surprise. "Nothing to complain about, anyway."

"Hmpf," he fiddled some with his reel.

He got like that sometimes, talking about things which seemed important to him but never really talking about them directly for fear of trespassing.

I cast my line out again, waiting.

"Guess it's kind of hard to meet — folks — out here sometimes."

"I do all right."

"Hmm... saw Jan Gregor last weekend, did you?"

Ahh, light dawns. "She was having a bit of a party and invited me over for it."

The tension in his bulky frame eased noticeably. "Good — good people, Jan is."

I nodded. "I'm doing fine, Jake. No need to worry."

He shifted a little, the huge old rowboat swaying gently with his weight. "Natural to worry. I know how isolated it can get to be around here."

"For more than myself, I'd bet," I allowed gently, thinking of him and Mrs. Stevens.

An eyebrow went up at that, and he looked at me consideringly. Then a broad sort of grin sprouted. "Well, there's always gossip-mongers creating rifts."

His gaze drifted north to the upper lake, nodding at that far-away point of the Standish summer house. "Haven't seen so much of your friend, Annabel, this summer. Everything all right between you two?"

I paid my attention to my fishing line. "I get over 'bout once a week."

"She coming to your party like usual?"

"No, they're heading back east early. Grandmama's seventy-fifth birthday is early in September, and there are arrangements to deal with. Apparently the whole family — from New York to Boston — is assembling."

"Hmm. I remember a time when you two saw each other nearly every day."

"We're not children anymore. Responsibilities do tend to take up time."

"That they do... maybe I work you too hard."

I laughed at that one. "You're talking in circles, Jake."

"Not the first time, I'm sure. Still, I don't want

you growing up any faster than you're ready for, Jenny. There's nothing wrong with enjoying a little of life instead of jumping straight into work'n'all. You want to be more of a hired hand for a bit — not so much a partner, you let me know."

"I would have said something sooner then this, if it was getting too much for me, Uncle Jake."

"Aye—" he cracked a grin, "being docile never was one of your strong suits."

I scowled at him good-naturedly, and together, our lines cast out.

"Did Beth mention she's thinking 'bout retiring?"

"You're joking? I can't see her slowing down for anything."

"Well," Jake shrugged, "not tomorrow-like, but in a couple years."

I took him more seriously, "What's that doing for you?"

He took his time in answering, reeling in his hook to find the minnow had come free and tending to the bait before me. The water went plop with his cast, and he clicked his reel latch down. "I've been thinking about traveling some."

"Oh?"

"Been here in Chautauqua since I was twenty-two, Wren. Things have changed some 'round this country. I'd like to see some of it, I think. Like to see a few other fishing spots too — been in this one long enough, you could say."

"It's been a while," I had to agree.

"Was thinking about one of those win'abaga-things, you know? Instead of a trailer? Just drive around and enjoy letting someone else be the guide — work a bit on my trout fishing."

I nodded, faintly. "Mrs. Stevens like to travel?"

"So-so... Beth's got grandchildren down in Florida, an' one out in California. Lot of fishing holes between here and California."

Strange, I didn't feel particularly threatened by the news, and I realized how much a part of me this place had become. Home just wasn't people-bound anymore, it was a place that held memories of loved ones... a place to keep the fires burning for their return.

"Mr. Henry was talking to me yesterday," I added after a minute. "His son's in Florida too. Apparently the boy's been after him to move down near him."

Jake nodded, "He gave notice this morning."

"How long?"

"August a year. He wouldn't want to leave us in a bind, you know."

I grinned, "Ought to be able to find a mechanic by end of next summer."

He tipped his head, half-shrugging, "Never can tell. Hard to find good people who are willing to settle down sometimes."

"Harder in Chicago than here, I'd wager."

"Yeah, folks don't usually go so very far here, even these days. But oh — I'll miss ole' Jay Henry. He's been with me for a good twenty years, now. Rarely complains, even when I saddle him with incompetent young fools like — oh, what was his name? Paul's older sib."

"Brian?"

"Yeah, a real handful. Henry always knew how to keep them in line, though, even when they were more interested in the skirts than the motor oil. He's a good man."

"Kind of like the changing of the guard," I murmured.

"How'd you figure?"

"Well, Mrs. Stevens, you — and Mr. Henry. The backbone of this place, wouldn't you say?"

"We ain't about to jump ship and leave you all together, kiddo. I haven't put this place together just to have it crumble up and blow away, because I dump it on you without experience."

"No, I didn't mean you would. Just—"

He nodded at my shrug, "It's coming to be your time — your place. Your own people to find and trust to the running of the lot. You'll do fine, Wren. You've got years yet to learn 'bout judging folks and working with them."

"Mrs. Stevens plans on retiring when, you say?"

"Three... four years — myself, I'd consider closer to five." He didn't look at me as he continued, "Maybe you already know someone who'd like working with that wood stove? Save the chaos of renovating and all."

"You mean Annabel." I shook my head. "She's doing just fine with her illustrations, and she has quite a household to run in Philadelphia."

"Seems to me," he pursed his lips, studying his hook that had let yet another minnow loose, "you could have been running quite a household in Chicago, if you'd gone the way your daddy wanted."

I remembered Dickie and that Edward person who was floating around in Annabel's other-life. But for once my protective instincts didn't flare. She was a woman who could take care of herself. I was coming to trust her to ask, when she needed help these days.

"We'll see," I shelved the questions. "As you said, there's plenty of time."

Chapter Twelve

Ms. Cassel, I do hope I'm not catching you at an awkward time?"

Dumbfounded I took Mr. Thomas' hand as Mrs. Stevens left, closing the study's door behind her. I felt my knees begin to fold. The edge of the desk chair scrapped my legs, and I sank back into my vacated seat.

"Yes, well—" He cleared his throat somewhat politely and glanced about, seating himself on the leather couch. "I realize this is probably a bit of a surprise—"

I closed my mouth with an effort. Surprise? Surprise?! Try shock!! Although we'd briefly exchanged letters regarding Annabel's artwork rights for the first of Quill's books, Mr. Thomas and I had never actually met as... well, as contemporaries.

"I — er, trust you remember me?"

"Ah — certainly, I do, sir." I pulled myself up straighter in my chair, depositing the nearly broken pencil on my ledger, and tried to make some coherent comment. "It's been what — a year-and-a-half since our correspondence regarding Annabel's contract?"

"Yes, yes," and he looked quite pleased with me.

He also looked very much the lawyer with his three piece, pin-striped suit and thinning dark hair. Gone were the white summer linens and Panama hat — and the hair tonic. The change in his appearance alone could have made him unrecognizable.

"I have here—" he opened the square, metal attaché he carried with his briefcase and pulled an antique jewelry box from it, "a present from the

Grandmama Standish."

"A — for me?"

He nodded succinctly, placing the box on the desk at my elbow and resuming his seat to retrieve a thick envelope from his briefcase.

"You are, I believe, turning nineteen in approximately two weeks?"

I nodded.

"Since Mrs. Standish will not be here at that time, she requested I present you with this now. She thought it might be best if it were to come through me, since any legal trivia could be ironed out before questions arise."

I swallowed hard and took a better look at the rectangular box beside me.

"Originally from Russia," Mr. Thomas was skimming through his briefs now, "this box is a lacquered antique from — unfortunately, an unidentified region at this date. Although, I assure you that I am still trying to trace its roots. The contents...?"

At his expectant glance, I hurriedly lifted the lid. But I found myself amazed at the silken texture of the lacquer beneath my fingertips.

"The contents are various pieces — including two broaches, a double string of pearls, the diamond and sapphire necklace with matching pin, earrings and ring."

Necklace?! It was more of a dancing waterfall, the silver filigree creating a shimmering net of the gems. It should have graced Annabel's neck... my breath caught with my mind's image of such magical beauty spilling down between her soft breasts.

"Mr. Thomas, I can't take these!"

He gave me a squashing look and merely

continued to read.

"I can't!"

"Do you concur that such pieces are present?" His thin brows were raised and he hadn't the slightest intention of dealing with my protests until his own duties were completed.

"Ah — yes...," although I'd missed at least half of his list.

"And these—" Mr. Thomas extended two envelopes, sealed with wax and tied in blue ribbon. "These you are not to open until *the appropriate time.*"

"Which is when?"

"Mrs. Standish assures me it will be quite a few months, if not years before you will need to read them. Will you abide by her wishes?"

I blinked. "Of course, I — certainly."

"Miss Annabel has informed me that you have an office safe on the premises. Is it adequate for holding such valuables? Or should I assist you in acquiring a safety deposit box?"

"Oh, no, there's room here... I can deal with a bank later if—" I swallowed hard and suddenly realized he wasn't about to listen to me at all. "Mr. Thomas, I can't accept these! These are Annabel's by rights. What on earth is Grandmama doing?!!"

"You will find, Ms. Cassel," he sighed shortly, already packing his things together again, "that Grandmama Standish is perfectly sane in most everything she has ever undertaken. She wishes you to have these things. She knows you'll appreciate them fully and hopes they will also offer a safeguard against any future monetary needs which may arise. She trusts that, should you have desired more immediate cash rewards, you would have already acquired them for yourself, as I understand your own resources are by no means small. The legalities have all been accomplished — the inheritance papers have been filed and the appropriate taxes paid." He handed me another envelope, this one stuffed overly thick, "Here are the details and appraised costs, along with suggested insurance policies. You may wish to have your own lawyers review these things before choosing a particular policy."

"Mr. Thomas," I interrupted quietly, yet firmly, "these things belong to Annabel. Not to me. And I don't want them."

"Yes, well I sympathize, but there is very little you can do about it at this point. I know you understand my meaning, when I remind you," he gave me a significant look as he got to his feet, "the matter has long been a dead issue."

"Understand you — yes!" I rose from my seat, stepping between him and the doorway. "But we both know it's not so simple either!"

"In the eyes of the legal system, Ms. Cassel, it is very simple. Quite frankly, there isn't much I can do at this point. If you refuse, you see — then the state will acquire the lot, since I'm afraid there is no one else at the moment to accept them. So I'd suggest," he smiled, suddenly much kinder and much less the officious estate executor, "that you take it up with Grandmama Standish yourself."

My mouth dried and my throat closed. Grandmama knew me well, and he had me. Never could I let these precious heirlooms carelessly pass into any stranger's hands.

"I see we do value the same concerns." He hesitated, then gently steadied me with a hand to my shoulder. "Will you be all right, Miss Jenny?"

From somewhere, I conjured up something of a

smile and a nod. "Yes, I will. Thank you, Mr. Thomas. Shall I see you out?"

"No need. Good day to you now."

"And to you, sir."

But deep within me, I felt my stomach tighten and the anger begin to boil. These weren't merely precious pieces of jewelry, Grandmama had presented to me... they were the wedding presents of her mother and grandmother, and her own — even her daughter's, Annabel's mother. A gift — even a generous one — I would have been flattered by, but this — this was part of Annabel's heritage, and it did not belong to me. It was Annabel's, regardless of her need to wear them in marrying this Edward or not. They were hers. And I had no intention of robbing her of a single piece of that lineage... not a single piece!!

* * *

"Your grandmother is impossible!" and the screen door slammed behind me as I stormed out into the night.

"Wren!"

My feet halted, and helplessly, my hands went up into the air. I couldn't do this to her — not again.

"Please Wren?" Annabel's voice was pleading as she too left the house, and I could feel her anxious gaze. "Don't leave angry—?"

With a deep breath of reluctance, I turned. My arms opened wide in a shrug. "I'm sorry."

Satin rustled as she made her way down the steps, the dusty blue of her dress melting into the shadows of the night. And I sighed again as she joined me.

"I do have to go."

"I know." Solemnly, she tucked a hand beneath my arm and we started for the boat. The satchel on my shoulder bumped a bit, and I felt incredibly weary as I settled the straps more securely; the jewelry box suddenly seemed very, very heavy. But then it was late too, well past midnight, and it was the last time I would see Annabel this summer. There was, perhaps, more than the jewelry fretting me.

"I did so want you to have a good time at your birthday dinner...?" Tears hovered at the edges of that quiet voice.

"I'm sorry," I repeated, squeezing her hand. "Saying good-bye is just so hard for me."

Annabel nodded mutely.

Muddled, I shook my head as the feeling of betrayal rose once more. "She has no right to do this to you!"

"Why do you keep saying that, Jenny?" she pulled me to a stop. Her face was earnest as she gazed at me, the moonlight freeing us to see one another now that we had come beyond the trees.

"Because by rights, this jewelry is yours, Annabel. It's been in your family for generations. These things shouldn't be given to — to some outsider with no cause or use to claim them. It isn't right."

"An outsider?" she echoed disbelievingly. "Is that who you think you are, Wren?"

"I — I'm not her granddaughter."

"No," she agreed quietly, "but neither are you a stranger. As for rights? Wren, these are Grandmama's to do with as she pleases. And it pleases her to give them to you."

"But why? I mean, she's never—"

"She has her reasons." Annabel smiled at the thought. "Grandmama always has her reasons."

"Do you know them?"

"Not specifically, but I know she loves you, Wren — that you're dear to her. And she knows this year is very special for you. This is the year you've come home to stay... to take your chosen place beside your uncle. This year you will not be returning to your hated Chicago. Perhaps she thinks of this time as your Coming of Age? I don't know.

"But I do know, this isn't about money or stuffy traditions. It's about trusting — and about love. She trusts you to cherish these tokens of family and hope. She trusts you to pass them on someday to another of your choosing. And she loves you enough to want to give you a blessing of beauty — a gift to remind you that you are not the outsider you proclaim to be."

I felt my throat tighten. How could I ever refuse such a gift? "Yet what about you?"

She took both my hands, "Make it our gift."

"It feels—" Torn, I stepped away, gazing out to that moonlit lake in search of answers. I turned to Annabel again, still struggling for words and sense. "I feel this a thief. Like — I'm cheating you."

"Never. You're not stealing anything, Wren. It's a gift of belonging — of loving. I'd never feel you cheated me of anything. How could I? Especially not when—" Annabel bit off her words, spinning away quickly as my heart missed a beat.

I jumped forward, catching her arm and holding her from escape. The satchel slipped to the ground, and I moved closer, barely finding the courage to press for what she'd meant to say.

"Especially not when what, Annabel?"

"Please Wren—" Her face was averted, hidden in the shadows of the trees.

"No—" I persisted quietly. "I want to know."

A ragged tremor passed through her, and I realized she was very nearly crying. Then her words came suddenly, rushed in a whisper of defeat, "Especially not when it's you."

"When it's me?" Relentlessly I shook her arm, demanding more, "Why—? *What* especially because it's me?!"

A half-shrug and, "Because I love you."

Time stopped. Then the world went into a spin as I dared hope for the first time in my life that she might mean what I meant.

"Please Wren, it's all right." She turned, trying to undo the words she'd said. "I don't mean for you—"

"No!" fear made me rash, "Say it again."

She looked at me in despair.

"Say it!"

"I love you...." It was less than a murmur.

"And I love you."

Worry — disbelief touched her expression.

"Didn't you know?" I grasped her shoulders. "It's always been you. But I never — I can't... please say I'm not misunderstanding. Please, Annabel... please—"

There were tears on her face as her hand lifted to touch my cheek. And it was as soft, as gentle — as warm a touch as I had ever imagined. My eyes closed, her palm cradling my face — and then I found myself staring wide-eyed at her again. Scarcely believing my senses as she tenderly brushed aside my hair. And her fingers drifted down, playing across my skin — pausing at my lips, until I caught them with a kiss.

"My dearest Wren—" and there was astonishment in her voice as well as her heart, "how could you not guess? I've loved you since before Europe. Since before you — how could you not know?"

"Know—?" I begged again, wanting so desperately to hear the words over and over and over.

Annabel's smile returned, adoring me with her eyes and voice as she answered my plea, "That I love you. You — my Jenny-wren — my dearest Heart — with all my heart."

"I couldn't know," my voice came hoarsely. My fingers began their own exploring of the gentle slopes of her cheekbones... the softness of her skin and hair. "I couldn't even wish — I love you that much."

Now it was her turn to beg, but not for reassurance as her eyes fell to my lips with her murmur, "How much—?"

And I took her invitation, taking the sweetness of her mouth with the gentlest caress I knew. Her arms slipped around me and we drew nearer, losing time as we melted into oblivion.

But time was not a friend to either of us tonight. I moaned as I held her tight, burying my face in the silky hair and whispering in her ear, "Don't make me leave."

"If there was a way...." She left it unsaid. Her arms only tightened with acknowledgment of our fate.

"Tell me you'll be back. I live in dread something will happen over the winter months, and I'll lose you."

"Never — not now." And we drew apart as she solemnly pledged, "I will be here for you, Wren. Somehow, I will be back... I will always come back."

"Next summer—?"

"Early," she pressed an urgent kiss to my lips. "I promise you, early."

"I'll watch the windows."

"I'll light the oil."

And with that pledge, I had to be content.

* * *

In the deepest, darkest corners of winter despair can creep into the most contented of lives, especially when holidays gather and the missing of dearest loves can grow so poignantly acute. But she had not left me completely forsaken this year. By some sixth sense, Annabel had left a present with Jake for me, and the Christmas Tree brought a sweetness to banish the loneliness for a time.

It was a picture of shimmering light across the lake, and at the dock's end, a lone guitar player bent in concentration. A watercolor of subtle hues and harmony, it gave me no hint of isolation as I gazed upon the single musician. Because, after all, the painter had been near.

And so it gave me courage to wait for her return.

The Tenth Summer
Chapter Thirteen

The porch door was propped open, a testimony to the unusually mild June we were having and probably in an attempt to air out that musty smell the house acquired each winter. But the temperature was beginning to drop as I arrived, and so I let myself in while closing the door behind me.

"Hello!" I felt welcomed by the familiar glow of the oil lamps, and my mouth watered with the scent of roasting meat.

"—Kitchen!" came my reply and I smiled foolishly at the mere sound of her voice.

I dropped my overnight bag at the foot of the stairs and left my bulky sheepskin coat on the banister. Catching a glimpse of myself in the hall mirror, my stomach did a flip-flop. I suddenly felt very exposed in my gray slacks and angora sweater; I should have worn the jeans.

"Hello yourself," Annabel's smile deepened as she greeted me from the stove. "It's good to see you, Jenny."

"Tis certainly that!" Mrs. Hodges seconded with fervor. "Here I was dreading Master Richard's come back for somethin' forgotten or other. Dear Mary 'n' Joseph, what a muddle he can make of a dinner! Is it any wonder Herself is needin' a nap?"

"Not to worry," Annabel's voice soothed, calming all fears of this evening being spoilt. "He's on the train and gone by now."

"And good riddance! He was more hindrance than help with the unpacking yesterday." Mrs. Hodges' knife went "chop" through the apple to underline the housekeeper's words.

"Was he—?" but I was barely listening. I didn't seem to be able to keep my eyes from Annabel. Her apron only partially hid the pearl silk and gray-blue taffeta of her long dress. Her hair was up in a soft knot, and her eyes met mine boldly. Her cheeks flushed as we stared, but it wasn't from the kitchen stove.

A wooden spoon lifted to her lips, and I felt jealous for an instant. Then her mischievous smile was beckoning to me as she called, "Come tell me what you think of the sauce, Wren."

I grinned even more foolishly and slipped my hands into my pockets to keep them out of trouble.

"Does it need more pepper? Or will that make it too spicy?"

My eyes never left hers as I bent to taste from that spoon. Her hand cupped my chin, feigning a need to catch stray drops but her slender fingers trailed, lingering — promising, and I felt an answering passion rise.

"Pepper or not?" she prompted, voice utterly calm and tinged with mere curiosity. It was her eyes which teased so mercilessly.

"No," I straightened, still holding her gaze. My mouth twitched with a wicked smile of my own, "there's more than enough pepper here."

Annabel appeared from behind me. She leaned low over the back of the sofa to peer at the book in my hands, then asked quietly, "Has Grandmama gone to bed?"

"Yes, a little while ago."

She looked at me then, those cinnamon eyes stealing my heart with her calm scrutiny. She was so close, the faint scent of lavender tempting me with the promise of softness.

"Will you come for a walk with me?" she asked. "Mrs. Hodges will be up yet for a bit—"

In answer I closed the book and stood to join her. I would have followed her anywhere she'd cared to go.

The evening had grown cool, but the stars were out, and her hand was warm as it slipped beneath my arm. I forgot the chill and felt the calm of my lake descend. It was such a beautiful night to spend with her.

Annabel smiled, squeezing my arm with silent understanding. In unison, we started down the steps.

"I like this sweater," she murmured, running her hand up and down my arm. "And the lack of blue jeans."

"I thought I might dress for dinner for a change."

"Hmm — Grandmama was impressed."

That startled me, "Was she?"

"Hm-hmm. She'd never say anything, naturally, but I heard her mention to Mrs. Hodges that you looked rather charming—"

I was glad it was dark as my face grew red with embarrassment. "I didn't mean to cause talk."

"You didn't," she assured me, smiling, "and I wouldn't care if you did."

"No," I was smiling in return, "I don't think you would."

We rounded the dividing line of trees, and she gestured towards the dim outline of the boathouse. The windows to her studio were glowing faintly in welcome, and she asked, "May I show you something?"

I nodded, and we wandered on in that direction.

"Have I told you how lovely your dress is?"

"No," she murmured, almost shyly.

"Or how lovely you look in it?"

She glanced at me then, "Thank you."

"I've missed you."

She nodded. "I was praying you would come — and dreading you might run into Dickie. He would have spoiled the whole day."

I shook my head, "I wouldn't have let him."

Her expression was grateful. "I'm glad you're here."

"So am I...."

The studio door was unlocked, and she let me in before her. Cozy heat from the fire greeted us, and her windows had been hung with thick lace to guard privacy. An oriental rug of turquoise and olive warded off the draft from the floorboards. A hope chest inlaid with flowers and an armoire with brass fastenings had come to join the easel and desk furnishings. The little brass bed was laid with a feather tick the color of dusky red roses, and invitingly, it was turned down to show the lace trimmed pillows and sheets.

And on the mantel, beside the small bed, the hand-carved jewelry box I had given her stood. Its lid was open and the gold locket dangled — a silent welcome to this, our special haven.

The door closed behind me, and I faltered, finding words beyond me to describe the preciousness of this place she'd created. Then words failed me in another cause as I turned to find her there.

She drew the pins from her hair, shaking the silken knot free unhurriedly, and my breath caught as her eyes held mine. She bent, lifting her skirts to place a foot upon the chair. Her hair tumbled around her, cloaking her as her fingers freed buttons and slipped off the one shoe. The other followed, and I thought my knees would fold as she reached beneath the taffeta breast panel of her dress.

"Sit down, Wren," her voice was a quiet, throaty timbre, and I obeyed weakly, sinking to the side of the bed.

The dress opened to the waist, allowing glimpses of a cream and pink-ribboned corset. Her head bent for a moment in concentration as she reached behind to undo the hooks and placket. The dress slipped from her and was laid in the chair. Her corset followed more slowly, freeing breasts of milky white and rose hue. Silk and lace pooled around her ankles, and without a word Annabel stepped from the last of her garments.

Her hands were gentle as they sank into my hair, tipping my face upwards — brushing past the softness of her breasts — to receive her kiss. Warm, and slow, and deeply we met — her mouth sweetness and mint... her waist silken and warmth beneath my hands.

I felt myself melting inside as she pulled the sweater and camisole from me, abandoning my kiss for only the moment it took to free me from the cloth. Then she was drawing me to my feet and smoothing more clothing from my waist and hips as she held me fast with her kiss.

Skin became satin as we melded together, and the silk of her hair swirled about us as she lowered me back to the bed. Legs entwined and we rolled as one, softness eclipsing all sense as we gasped for breath and held to each other tightly.

Lavender would haunt me with memories of this night, I thought, breathing in her very beauty with the scent. I groaned, burying my face into the warm nest of her shoulders and hair. I felt her sigh as she arched to keep the length of us close.

"Dear God in heaven...," I murmured, lifting myself to see her, brushing the hair gently from her face — kissing the ivory hand that stroked my freckled shoulder with such a loving touch.

"You are so very beautiful," she whispered, her eyes wide and marveling at the play of her own hands across my skin — at the tender line of my face as I looked down at her. "I'd forgotten how very beautiful..."

"For you," I insisted quietly. "I am made for you—"

She smiled then, fingers touching, tracing the shape of my face... the corners of my mouth. And I clasped her hands in my own, pressing kisses to those dear fingertips and smiling, because she was pleased.

"I love you," she breathed.

I nodded, her hands still held to my lips, "Almost as much as I love you."

A disbelieving sparkle lit in the depths of her eyes, but she did not argue. And I smiled even more, until the beauty of her — of what we were about to share overcame me again. Then moments became eternity, and I could do no more than stare — than hold her. With patience, she cherished our stillness, her gaze adoring me in return, and we found no need for hurry.

"You are lovelier than I have ever imagined," I managed hoarsely. "And I have imagined you a thousand different times...."

Again, I had pleased her, and her fingers played upon the swollen softness of my lips.

"You do know—" she whispered quietly, the merest hint of her more practical ways mingling with her sweet mischief, "I don't have the faintest idea of what I'm doing?"

"Don't you?" I caught her teasing fingers lightly between my teeth. But I relented quickly and kissed her fingertips again, tender now with reassurance. "I don't think it will take long to change that."

She nodded, pulling me down to kiss again, and her hands slipped around me, smoothing the planes of my back — dissolving my skin with utter softness. Her lips drifted across my face, her tongue moist and tasting the form of my eye — the arch of my brow. And then her fingers were spreading wide and joining her lips' caress in my ruddy-brown hair.

"Oh—" her breath was warm as she buried her face in my hair, "I love it so short.... The way it feels between my fingers... so light and soft...."

"For you—" I murmured, finding the velvet hollow of her throat with my own lips. And she arched as gently I devoured the milky length of her neck — tasting the creamy hue of her skin with my circling tongue.

Our hands... our mouths explored, coaxing desires and flushing our skin bright. My touch was — gentle, almost reverent, as my lips took her firm, round breasts to pleasure them... her passion rising, demanding abandoned response as she claimed mine. Then I reached to the smoothness her thighs as she straddled me. No longer to be denied, my hand sought her moist nest. Hair so fine, curls lush in wetness... my fingers slowed, savoring the delicateness of unfolding, and she gasped. She bent to bury her face in my shoulder, and I heard her sweet "yes — please" as I found her.

She trembled, biting me quickly then breaking off, kissing the offended skin and amending, "I'm sorry."

"It's all right," I murmured, dipping gently now into her — swirling and beckoning her to move with me. "Climb my Love—"

And with a moan of long, low rapture she pushed into my hand.

I held her nearer, raking my teeth lightly — then greedily taking her breast as her hands sank again into my hair. Gasping for breath, she pushed, writhing — dancing for me in loving.

"Ohhh... dear heavens—" A groan stole from her throat and her hips pulled away uncertain, before again seeking my touch, I lifted my head kissing farewell to her tender, reddened breast, and she groaned again, the rhythm suddenly lost in her thrusting movements.

"Too much?" I ventured, gentle with whisper, as my fingers yielded slowly.

A sob or a gasp and a nod returned, her eyes closed to me.

"There's more," I murmured, my hand cupping her sweetness — warm and soothing as I turned us, guiding her beneath me. "A gentler more—"

Her eyes opened wide to watch as my mouth began a tender, downward trail.

My gaze smiled at her as my lips sank into her moistness. Curls as fine as pure down to the touch — heady mingling of musk and lavender... warm wetness... exquisite, tasting beyond delight, I found her again — and in a gentler way. My eyes slid shut as I lost myself — the longing... the wanting... the sweetness of her coming more precious than any winter dream had ever been.

It was her turn now as she lay me out, hands flowing gently across my slight breasts — my hips and thighs. Her turn it was now to take the slowness of discovery... the tentative touch of such intimate exploring... to bring me near, rising in yearning, aching need. And her hands grew surer... her mouth more avid, and I felt the soles of my feet burn white as senses eclipsed in a cry.

I was hers....

Her silken hair wrapped around us as I held her close. The dark rose quilt drew over us both, and with a single sigh we settled still for a time.

And I knew, too, that she was mine.

Chapter Fourteen

This is killing me," Annabel murmured.

Startled, I looked up from my place at her breast, thinking the humor had been there for me to hear, but her eyes were shadowed with seriousness. I frowned, covering her gently with a sheet as I drew up beside her. The day had been idyllic in its fashion, or so I'd thought, with the sunlight pooling in the middle of the studio despite the heavy lace curtains, and the passion we'd shared had been touched with such tenderness.

"I see you so seldom," she supplied, frustration brimming to tears in her eyes. "Does it seem I want so much? Just to look out a window and to see you sanding a hull or pass a door to see you at a desk — to know you'll be there at the day's end? I feel like my heart is torn from me with every hour spent in goodbyes."

My throat ached, and I could not bear to say I should ever leave again if it made her feel this way. My mind raced in its circles of desperate fears. Solutions were so few here.

"Is it different for you?"

Her vulnerability echoed in those words, and I was quick to shake my head to reassure her. "No, Love. It's no different at all. But—"

Annabel lifted my chin, drawing my eyes back to hers. "But?"

"You have more courage, I think. I barely dare to believe how much we do have."

"That makes you content?" Her voice was disbelieving.

"It makes me frightened of losing what little we

do have — of losing all I've never dared hope for that unbelievably we do have!"

Her eyes sparked with quiet fury. "It is not enough."

I swallowed hard, scorched by the passion of her determination. And I found a way, "Then come work for me."

She blinked. It was her turn to be puzzled.

"Mrs. Stevens retires in a couple seasons. We're half-looking for her replacement already — an excuse to see if you'd like the work? Come spend the summer on my side of the lake."

"And Grandmama?"

It was not an idyll question nor one of permission. Grandmama had been quite ill with influenza over the winter months, and her frailty still lingered. It seemed she had grown older in these past six months than in the total of her previous seventy-odd years.

"She says she's well. You've said the same. Perhaps, she's less able to go without a mid-day nap and less prone to midnight seances, but all else is well. And Mrs. Hodges is always here, often with the day maid... or have you been misleading me about her health?"

Annabel's fingers pressed the suspicion back to my lips, her eyes earnest as she shook her head. "I would not lie to you, Wren. Not now."

"I know." I kissed her palm, taking her hand in my own, "I'm sorry. I — I just had this sudden, horrible thought of your trip to Europe and your silence — of that silence happening all over again."

"It won't." Her face grew tender and she kissed me gently, lingering with soft comfort, "We plan to be here next summer, Dearest. I've no intention of disappearing on you."

"And yet you scold me for each time we must part?" Now that she had tempted me with such possibilities, I was loath to let the hope go. "If I am to kill you, Beloved, come let it be from unending nights of pleasure! And from days of holding you within sight. Come work for me!"

She was tempted.

"You know the workings of Mrs. Stevens' wood stove. That's rare these days. So it would make sense for you to be thinking about taking on her lodge job, when she retires. There's no reason anyone would question us closely."

"No one at all?" Her suspicions were piqued.

"No one of any consequence. Who do you hear complaining of Jake and Mrs. Stevens? None who any of us call friends. And neither Jake nor Mrs. Stevens would ever stand against us." I suspected she only half-believed me. "Okay then, we'll get you your own room."

Her brows lifted in jest.

"I   will!!   There's   the   one   adjoining   my bathroom—"

"Your storage room?" She was laughing now.

"It used to be a bedroom, a good sized one. The light would be good for your painting—?" I grinned then. Finally I'd caught her attention.

Her tongue moistened her lips. She was still hesitant.

"Whole nights with me," I murmured, taking her in my arms to press my body against the silky length of hers. "Nights in a bed with no springs, no interruptions... no one being inquisitive. And there are locks on my doors."

Annabel blushed. We both remembered only too

well the near disaster of Mrs. Hodges' generous offer of a tea tray one night; she had been concerned because of "how restless" we'd sounded.

"Oh Wren," her eyes held a glimmer of excitement, "I don't dare...."

But in the end, she did... and with Grandmama Standish's full blessings.

* * *

I sighed, rubbing the sweat from my eyes with the back of a fishy hand and wondered when this weather would break. The cloud ceiling was thick, but the glare burnt through, threatening to freckle my skin even worse than it was. We'd had several cases of blistering sunburn from our fishing guests too. Although this weather was typical for a week or two any summer, this year's torture seemed to be persisting beyond all reason.

Quit moaning, I told myself as I picked up the garden hose again to finish scrubbing down the outdoor countertop. It was decidedly better to be skinning fish in the shade than sitting out on the lake doing a slow, reflective bake. And since I'd just finished the last of the catch and could look forward to a quick hop in the shower, what was I complaining about?

My hands, I thought, feeling those little clear scales clinging and biting into my skin as I snapped the garbage lid down on the last of the fish innards. It had never been much a concern to me before — the skinning and filleting. I had been doing it for so many years that the chop-slit-and-slice process was like sleepwalking. And to be fair, I was a whole lot more nimble at it than Jake was, so I was the logical choice for the job on most days.

Fish scales, however, did a lot scraping and chafing on the skin, and my hands were the texture of sandpaper whenever I finished. The cold water clean-ups never helped either. Fortunately, hand lotion did, and the damage was never permanent.

The clatter of dishware and the familiar laughter drifted through the windows above me. Murmurs of conversation floated to me as Annabel and Mrs. Stevens finished the last of the lunch dishes and began the preliminary dinner chores.

I found myself smiling quite unexpectedly, remembering why my hands had become so important to me.

It was turning into such a lovely summer. I ducked my head under the icy stream of the hose, purring with relief at the cold water's touch. Despite the shade of the overhanging maples, my skin felt fried, and reluctantly I admitted I really should find a hat to wear one of these days.

A foot scuffled and a polite cough interrupted me. I straightened, to find Paul of all people.

He nodded a bit awkwardly and remembered his cowboy hat, snatching the battered straw thing from his head. He ran a hand through his light hair as he nodded again, "Hello Wren — Jenny."

I pulled the bandanna from my pocket and absently dried my face, too surprised to say much.

"Ahh—" the hat waved towards the beach around front or somewhere, "they said Jake was out — that I should see you."

I smiled suddenly, remembering this not quite shy, not quite assertive pose of his. "It's good to see you again, Paul," and I meant it. "What can I do for you?"

He relaxed visibly and let out a grin. "It's good to see you too. How you been?"

"Fair," I mused, then allowed, "More than that really. How 'bout yourself? Still over at Cummings?"

"I'm doing all right," he slid his fingers along the brim of his hat. "Actually, Cummings is what I'm here about."

"Oh?" I shut the water off, prepared to listen.

"It's pretty good work'n all," he shrugged, "but being indoors — factory line, it's hard in a different way."

I nodded, "I couldn't do it."

"Yeah, well — I heard Jay Henry's thinking on leaving you all, and I was wondering if you've got anybody to take his place yet?"

"No one in particular. You interested?"

Paul admitted it with a crooked sort of grin, "Very."

Arms folded, I looked him over for a minute.

"You know my work." He gave a shrug, looking off towards the lake. "You know I can squeeze life out of most any boat motor. I've been doing some night work too, down at Pickert's in Bemus. So I've kept my hand in and can do pretty well with trucks'n'cars now too."

I grinned. Paul had a habit of underselling his talents. If he said "pretty well," he was probably working miracles.

"Weak point's still the same. Electrical wiring'n'all. I don't know how I'd do at keeping the guest cabins up to par on their lighting."

"Would you be willing to take some classes?"

"Sure." He nodded, that hat pointing south this time, "There's some night courses down at the community college this fall. I've got the pre-requisites already."

"Done your homework for this, haven't you?"

"Yeah, guess I have."

"Good enough," I allowed and settled back against the stoop's banister, eyeing him closely. "Now tell me this. What about the pay cut? And why?"

"Truth is, I don't like the assembly line. I'm just not cut out for indoors and piecework. I'm dying in there, Jenny. And the only way out is out." He shrugged again, "I've been looking. Problem is, I don't want to go too far. And there's only so much call for garage mechanics... so here I am. This is what I do best, you know that. And it's the place I do it best — outdoors."

"And the money?"

"Your uncle don't pay all that bad, Jenny Cassel," he reminded me, a bit chagrined. Then he looked at me evenly, "It still a full-time, year 'round position?"

I nodded. "Room and board during the season, but you've got to fare food for yourself rest of the year."

"And the gatekeeper's house up by the road comes with it?"

Again I nodded, "Same as Jay Henry has."

His hat juggled a bit as he chewed something over in his mind, before, "Any objections to roommates?"

I shrugged, "Can get pretty lonely out here for a ladyfriend."

That was an understatement. The gate house was a small, two-bedroom cottage separated from the lodge and cabins by a long, dense line of fir trees and half an acre of concord grapevines. The road to civilization on the other side wasn't much more promising; this was farm country mostly, but aging farm country. So usually folks drove off for a full-time job in the morning, only to come home and cut hay, milk cows or tend grapes late in the day.

"That's another problem," I added at his silence. "Granted, the salary isn't bad, but it's not enough to support a family on, Paul."

He cleared his throat with a decided awkwardness. "I'm not really lookin' to have one."

"Wren—?" The inside screen door slammed behind me. I turned already smiling as Annabel crossed the boot room calling, "Are those fish ready for the freezer yet?"

Annabel paused at the outer door, surprised to find company. But she smiled readily as she recognized him. "Paul, how nice to see you again!"

"You remember Annabel?" I asked as she came out to join us.

"Sure do," Paul took her hand with a broadening grin. "And I'm flattered to find myself remembered."

"Of course you are," her voice warmed, setting him at ease. "How is your friend, Peter? Is he still around?"

"No, 'fraid not. He took off on the rodeo circuit, if you can believe that."

"Not one of those bronc busters?"

"Sure is."

"Paul's here about Mr. Henry's job," I supplied for her. "We were just talking about the drawbacks of the living arrangements—"

"Which she seems to think I should be concerned about," Paul inserted with a sheepish smile. "Jenny seems to think it's too isolated."

"Oh, I don't know about that." Annabel turned her teasing smile onto me, "You do well enough for yourself, Miss Cassel."

"We were talking about roommates and ladyfriends," I amended with dignity.

Annabel looked at Paul with a sort of surprised, questioning gaze, and he shifted his footing a bit. "Actually, I was jus' saying I don't particularly plan on being a family man, so the pay's certainly good enough. The location'n'all isn't really so much of a problem either."

"And roommates?" She directed the question to me. "You've objections there?"

I shook my head slightly, confused by this subtle air of challenge for her. "I was merely thinking it gets kind of lonely for a girl on her own out here. I mean, the summer season only lasts so long."

"Well, I—" Paul coughed and went on, "I wasn't thinking in terms of girlfriends, just — a roommate. And I'd certainly expect him to have a job of his own."

"Might be nice to have more neighbors around, Wren," Annabel noted, "especially in the winter. I worry about you and Jake getting stranded out here in the snow."

"Which is another advantage," Paul jumped in quickly. "Jay Henry's kind of agreed to pass on his truck and plow to the next fella. There's a fair piece of winter cash to be made in snow plowing and towing contracts."

That was true. Come winter, driveways always needed serious plowing on a regular basis. Four feet of snow just did not move with a shovel.

"Well, it's been good to you again, Paul. But you'll have to excuse me — I need to get those fish into the freezer."

Startled, I remembered what she'd come for and passed her the platter of saran-wrapped fillets.

As she disappeared into the house, Paul ventured a tentative guess, "She a regular now?"

"Kind of," I admitted with a faint smile. "For the summer at least. I don't know if she'll be talked into it again next year."

He bobbed his head, swallowing hard. But he didn't say anything.

As a matter of fact, he stopped looking at me altogether.

And suddenly, finally — in thinking of Annabel and watching him — I realized what Annabel had been challenging me on. As usual, I found myself mused at my own stupidity.

"Well, is there something else I can tell you—?"

I grinned abruptly, "Just promise continued discretion if you move in."

He looked up, surprised at my teasing tone, then broke out with that crooked grin of his. "This means I'm in?"

Growing serious, I sighed and moved forward a step or two. "How would you feel about being part-time for the rest of the summer and a final say in September? Give Jay Henry a chance to see how far you've developed, give yourself a bit of a look to be sure you really want to come back... give us all a chance to get used to each other again."

He settled his hat, pursing his lips some as he looked off towards the lakefront. "Could we work it around my shift at Cummings?"

"My thoughts exactly."

"How many hours?"

I shrugged, "Fourteen to twenty? Choose what's good for you and have Jay Henry write out a schedule for us."

Paul eyed me sideways, "You're being serious

here?"

"I am." My brow lifted with an honest humor, "But I'm not speaking for Jake."

His gaze dropped as the toe of his sneaker nudged at a rock. "It true that you're coming on as Jake's partner?"

"It's true. August makes it official."

He nodded and pushed the hat back a ways on his head. He looked very satisfied.

"Sound good?" I prompted.

"Yeah," and he grinned, thrusting out a hand to seal it. "Sounds real good."

I sent him off to unearth Jay Henry and wandered into the house, wondering at the quirks of fate.

"Well—?" Annabel accosted me in the kitchen, potato peeler in hand.

"Well what?"

Her eyes widened in exasperation, and I relented. "We're going to give it a go. 'Til the end of summer, he'll be part-time — and then we'll see."

Her face softened into a smile, a caress more tender than any kiss, and she approved, "Well done, Bosslady."

I chuckled, "Tell me that after Jake's grilled me."

She squeezed my wrist reassuringly, before going onto to other things. "It's almost three-thirty. You wanted reminding that the brochure agent's coming by about four."

"Yeah," I glanced about the adjoining doorways to make sure the coast was clear and brushed a kiss across her cheek. "Thanks—"

I think I left her smiling.

Chapter Fifteen

Annabel started awake, half rousing me from sleep. My arm tightened securely, reassuringly about her waist.

A faint knock registered through my daze. Somewhere a distant voice was asking something. But I knew that voice. It was only Mrs. Stevens.

Annabel moved again, as if to scurry from bed, and I pulled her firmly back to my side.

"Wren—" she hissed.

"Hush," I warned, and she stilled, recognizing I was awake. I smiled faintly, whispering, "Wait—"

She glanced over my shoulder at footsteps in the hall, then her eyes widened in disbelief as she noticed the clock. "You forgot to set—!"

"Shhh!"

The knock came again, a casual rap. This time it was at my door.

"Laundry day, Lazy Bones," Mrs. Stevens cheerfully called. "You want sheets and towels done, get'm down by nine o'clock, kiddo!"

The floorboards creaked and the dull, distant thumps on the back staircase followed. Sleepily I raised a smug brow, quite proud of myself. "See? No fire alarms — it's our day off. Remember?"

A slow anger gathered in her and her scowl darkened to a mutinous fury. "Don't you ever do that to me again! Do you hear me, Jennifer Cassel? Never again!"

"I don't—"

"I am not some Trovoli Square whore to be manhandled! And you do not rearrange my life without so much as a word to me!"

"I — I didn't... isn't your door—?"

"Yes!" she hissed. "My door is locked. Yes! Your door is locked. That is not the issue. But I had planned to help with the extra pastry orders this morning, and I do not like the idea of breaking my word simply because you didn't think to ask before resetting our alarm clock!"

"I'm sorry—" I felt miserable.

"And furthermore! I resent an iron-lock on my person because you think you know what's going on when you don't!"

"I'm sorry," I repeated, feeling much too vulnerable for this kind of argument so soon after waking.

"Oh Wren—" her voice softened and the angry mantel dissipated. "I just can't — please, ask me first?"

I nodded, fighting the tears and hating myself for threatening to cry.

Her fingers brushed the hair across my forehead. Then adoring and exasperated all at once, she looked down at me. "My poor, Wren. You're not even awake yet."

"I won't do it again," I murmured, holding her gaze the best I could.

"No," her laughter was warm and kind, "I don't expect that you shall."

And she had me laughing suddenly, her arms slipping around me to hold me close. I felt safe and loved again... her warm satin skin wrapping about me in exquisite care.

"Better?"

I nodded, receiving her kiss with a lingering sigh, until my eyes popped open and I abruptly asked, "What extra pastries?"

She smiled, pleased to know I truly had been listening. "The fresh apple delivery was this morning — Beth and I were going to get a head start on the pies to freeze and on the canning. We wanted to have some of it done before the afternoon heat set got too much."

I frowned faintly, "Pearsons' shipment is in?"

"It is. They called yesterday to say they'd be by this morning."

I shook my head hesitantly, "I don't think they made it."

"No?"

"They're usually here about five a.m. or six. Aren't they?"

She nodded, "Promised five-thirty at the latest."

"I don't think they made it. I mean, I always wake up when the delivery trucks come down our gravel drive, and I don't think I heard them this morning."

"Well," Annabel's eyes lit with mischief, "you did have rather a late night of it last night, Dearheart."

I purred as her hands possessively slipped down my waist, bringing memories of our midnight escapade. She took pity on me, stopping, and I gave up a reluctant sigh. "But habits are hard to break—"

"Oh?" A teasing eyebrow lifted as she tossed her loose braid over her shoulder. "So now I'm a habit, am I?"

I laughed, cuddling near and denied, "Nothing of the sort. I'm was talking about trucks and waking up."

"Well," her fingers played in my hair, "it would get you off the hook nicely, I admit."

"Never," I wiggled closer, grinning up at her from the softness of her shoulder. "I never want to be loose. I am happily, contentedly caught and blithely intend to stay that way."

"Are you really? And I suppose I have no say in the matter?"

I groaned in mock exasperation, my lips following the smooth, subtle curves down below her neck — my hand drifting up slowly to capture her breast.

"Ohh... sweet Mother of God!" She stretched lazily, deliberately — with hands reaching above her head, and the movement brought her taut nipple into my mouth.

I moaned at the taste of her — at the delight that tingled in my toes as she shivered. And then her hands were in my hair, pressing me nearer — urging a more avid assault. My fingers sought her other breast, tips grazing her rosy peak ever so lightly.

She took my wrist suddenly, halting my teasing touch. Then more gently, her palm pressed to my cheek in a silent request.

Pausing, I looked at her with my unspoken question. And she was beautiful to look at, with her pink blushed skin and seductively half-closed eyes. But her eyes widened even as I was melting and her resolve firmed. With one succinct word, she ended it all.

"Laundry."

Glancing at the clock, I flopped over onto my back with a different sort of moan. We had less than twenty minutes to shower, dress and get things downstairs.

"I hate you," I muttered, feigning viciousness. "All that sordid, perverse — unholy — practicality!"

She giggled and leaned over to plant a kiss on my nose. "Come along my deprived little saint, and I'll see what I can rustle you up for breakfast."

I looked skeptical.

"French toast?"

I grimaced and pulled myself out of bed. "Bribery, sheer bribery."

"Whatever works—"

* * *

I came to bed late that night, wondering vaguely what was to become of me if I was actually choosing account books over a nice, cozy embrace. But Annabel had only laughed softly and assured me it would do her no harm to crawl into bed by herself for a change.

Yet the night had become one of those fairy tale sorts, and I found myself drawn to my bedroom window. Turning off the bathroom lights, I pulled my robe more securely around me and opened the windows to the lake breeze.

The air was cool and sweet-smelling. It drifted across the calm, silver-laced waters and seemed to taste of magic. The shimmering lake was so black that the stars themselves dotted its glassy surface. The moon was high and full, and it was so close—

A hand touched my shoulder, warm in its loving clasp. "It seems like you could reach out, and find it right there in your grasp."

I nodded, then half-turned in concern. "I didn't mean to wake you."

Annabel nodded towards that shining marvel again. "Always wake me for this."

We stood there for the longest time. My arms slid about her waist as she leaned back into me, and we just watched the pale blue of the clouds drift past that great, round moon. The night seeping in around us, embraced us with its gentle coolness.

"I think," Annabel began from somewhere far off, "I understand now what Grandmama was so often trying to tell Dickie."

A tender surprise drew my attention to her.

"When my parents died, Dickie blamed the moon for their accident."

I hugged her slightly closer. Her parents' death was something she seldom spoke about.

"He blamed a lot of things actually — romance, magic... foolishness. But the moon—? He always seemed to focus on that glowing orb." She seemed to drift away for a while, and it took some time before she continued.

"My father was just as much the romantic as Grandmama, I believe. I remember he once said, Mama was 'as beautiful as the starlight' to him.... Grandmama still says, Mama brought 'the roses of winter to life' the night she danced into Papa's arms that night. It seems they never stopped dancing. After twelve years, he would still change when she walked into a room — still stand out of marvel and tenderness. His crisp, totalitarian air would dissolve like mist in the sunlight, and he would cease to breathe at the very sight of her."

Her hands slipped down over mine where they held her waist. We both knew that feeling all too well for ourselves.

"How they loved the moonlight, Wren. Papa loved to pamper Mama with midnight strolls and picnics in the wilds. Grandmama teased him, when he began to attend the late night, garden seances simply because Mama delighted in them so.

"Grandmama always remembers their happiness, I think. Whereas Dickie — Dickie mostly remembers their leaving. He still thinks they were irresponsible risking any kind of midnight outing on the river, no matter how calm the waters nor slow the current seemed.

"We were on Rhode Island somewhere, I remember that much of it for myself. We were staying with friends for a summer respite. And the moon was full.... Dickie says, they weren't to be swayed. They went boating — a picnic of cheese and wine, of love and moonlight upon the water.

"He's never forgiven them for not coming back, but Grandmama — in all her pain, she never said a bitter word. At least not in my hearing. Instead, she said it was a thing to find some hope in. They had died beneath the moon's magic... just as they had met that night in the courtyard ball. It was as if the very magic of Heaven had reached down to entwine their spirits and bind them together in their love with star dust — bind them beyond death with moonlight.

"Here tonight, seeing the moon and water dance like this—" she nodded again at the beauty of sky and the shimmering lake, those waters lapping so quietly against the shore. "I can understand what Grandmama meant. Before I was too young, Dickie's bitterness too sharp... but now?"

She moved to face me within the circle of my arms. Her eyes, dark in the room's shadows, rose to meet mine, and I felt an answering desire rise in me.

Then for the first time since I'd met her, I used the strength I'd gained in sanding hulls and swimming rough waters to lift her. Her arms slipped about my neck as I moved, her body warm and inviting through the nightgown. Her lips grew soft and yielding as I laid her amidst the streams of moonlight on our bed.

She lay still. Eyes wide, she watched as I slid

the robe from my shoulders, watched as I knelt beside her to unfasten the buttons at her throat... watched with breath growing shallow beneath my silent, promising stare.... My hands came to her, stripping the thin flannel from her body.

Naked — waiting, she laid unmoving, trusting the gentleness of my touch as I drifted, stroking — following the shape of her arms where they lay above her head. My hands returned — cupped, fitting the swelling beauty of her breasts, rubbing slowly in widening circles — drawing the firmness of desire into her nipples. And my palms tingled with the fires kindling brighter within myself. Her waist — she shuddered as my touch trailed, fingers playing in long, slow patterns — palms smoothing in warm, full possession. I bent, feeling the length of her thighs beneath my hands. My wrists and arms pressed her legs together as my breasts, taut with aching awareness, brushed across her knees, and then trailed further — softly dragging higher until each in its turn found her soft, curling hair to press against.

My mouth descended — moist and hungry to the trembling beauty of her waist — inflamed by her quivering arousal, so different in her stillness from the tigress lover I knew so well. Her breath was coming in short gasps as her fingers — her hands found my shoulders. And I held her beneath me... willing her to let me continue even as her legs stirred, half-seeking to push me from atop her.

The spell broke with a yearning cry as my mouth took her breast. Her hands sank into my hair, and she arched, pushing into me even as I held her from escape. But it was not escape from my touch she sought as her body strained to meet my skimming hands — her breasts, my greedy tongue.

"Now—" she murmured, need aching in her call. "Please Wren — now... ohhh"

And she discovered another way I could call the stars from her as with my mouth to her breast, my hands at her wrists above her head and my legs binding hers closely together — she lifted us both from the bed in a single thrust... and she fell as my mouth gentled and my legs relented.

Softness returned to replace tension, hands shook as they slipped into my hair, and I gathered her near, tender in my arms. I felt her still trembling, so faint — so very deep as I traced the corners of her eyes with my tongue and feather-light kisses. But the soft line of her lashes, the flushed caress of her silken cheek beneath mine stirred my need to seek another place of soft hair — taste a silkiness of another kind. My lips sank into her tousled mane. My tongue wet the swirl of her ear, and very, very quietly, I promised, "There is more... a gentler more."

She turned away slowly even as she opened to me. A moan of rapture — of melting pleasure bid me welcome even as her arms released me. Her thighs parted.

My fingers sought her first, cupping lightly as I kissed her flushed shoulder. She shuddered almost violently at my careful touch, but her hips moved then, circling slowly with the wetness I drew upon. And my mouth watered with urgency as I kissed her hips and thighs and inhaled the heady, heated brew.

"Oh, my Beloved...," I moaned as I grew drunk on the mere sweetness of her scent.

Her hands pulled me forward then, her hips lifting to urge my possession, and I found her opening beneath my tongue's caress... her lovely, heavy dew tasting of warm honey and unnamable wine. I groaned her name as I made her mine again — giving and loving and wanting no other thing save for this sweet scented drink.

She came suddenly, quickly beneath my tongue's gentle assuaging. And she came long and strong, waves washing through her and through her and through and beyond — her thighs in my hands, held to my face as I felt her orgasm reach to surround me.

A long, final shudder eclipsed the rest — bringing her legs and shoulders to tighten, nearly curling her knees to breast.

As her legs fluttered still, I felt my own coming in the gentler wash of a deep contented release. I found myself purring, arms holding moist thighs to my face. I wondered that I ever forgot just how sweet her scent is... how lovely her taste — and yet I must, because each time seemed so startlingly exquisite... that somehow I found I must have — did indeed, somehow forget.

"Come hold me," she whispered, and I rose to crawl up beside her.

Her eyes were heavy-lidded in her pleasure, and she took me into her arms. For a time we gave little more than a look, a touch drifting across a cheek — a finger brushing aside a wisp of hair.... Contentment and nearness added charms of their own.

Annabel smiled slowly, "I felt you follow...?"

I purred, satisfied as sleep tempted me — or that peaceful, sated limbo of half-wakefulness.

"Can you love me so much?"

"How could I not?" I murmured then.

Her hand cupped my cheek. In a possessive touch, she brought my chin up and my eyes widened.

"There is more—" she warned, her gaze burning

me as she turned my words about. "There is more —
but not a gentler more...."

I found the return of my beloved tigress, her
lips parting mine in fervored demand. I gasped as her
hand sought my breast with fire — and skill... and I
yielded as she bid.

Chapter Sixteen

I sighed heavily, pausing at the foot of the dock to study Annabel where she sat on that distant bench. The late August sun caught the golds in her hair as she bent her head to work upon the sketch in her lap. But her concentration was divided, and it was barely a moment before she was again, worriedly, casting her gaze outward.

Our visit here to Grandmama had yielded this melancholy. The cough which the older woman had never really been free of since the winter had worsened to a nasty cold. She was recovering already, Mrs. Hodges was quick to point out, and for a change, Grandmama was being quite sensible about resting. But I had felt the concern along with Annabel and Mrs. Hodges. Grandmama's skin had always held a warm, satin tone and her grey eyes a sparkle of merriment — unless crossed. Yet both were fading now beneath this new frailty, and I felt the impending loss as acutely as Annabel in some ways.

To be reminded of death is seldom pleasant. It's even less so, when it approaches one you love. Grandmama... she was well now, but her mortality was becoming more and more tangible.

And then again, there was the knowledge that the time Annabel and I had together was probably as finite as Grandmama's own life.

Annabel heard my approach along the dock boards and began to pack away her inks.

"Mrs. Hodges is back," I explained quietly, halting still a bit behind her.

"Grandmama continues to sleep?"

I nodded, then realizing she couldn't see me

answered, "Yes."

"We should go then. Beth may be needing help with the dinner...."

But neither of us moved towards the boat. We both knew Mrs. Stevens wasn't expecting us for a while.

I felt Annabel's sigh more than I heard it and came closer to lean over the bench back, sliding my arms around her shoulders and hugging her. "What is it you're thinking, Love?"

A hand squeezed my arm gratefully, but her answer was slow in forming.

My grasp tightened in reassurance.

"I was thinking about choices."

I nodded, my cheek to her hair.

"She has always taught me life is made of choices, and I am to be true to myself in my choosing. But—" Annabel broke off with a sad shake of her head. "Some things I do not see as choices, Wren. I know somewhere they must be, but not for me. They simply are as they are. I — could not change them."

"I know that," I straightened, coming to sit beside her as I took her hand. "I don't expect there to be a choice here."

Her gaze beseeched me for forgiveness, and I shrugged, my smile etched with melancholy, "She raised you, Annabel. She's given you everything from love to art — she is family in the truest sense of the word. You wouldn't be who you are, if you weren't prepared to return that faith — that love to her as she needs it."

"Still...," she looked at our hands as our fingers entwined, "I feel guilty about hurting you."

"I'm not asking you to choose," I promised, holding tight.

"You would have every right to."

"Do you think so?" An ironic, sadness twisted my lips. "And just what would I be demanding? That you be torn between the two women you most love in all this life? That you forsake the very one who brought us together? Should you risk losing both of us because you abandon her and — should I assume you can even stay here, with me, when you're beyond her power?

"And I am not that cruel, Beloved. At least," I amended, "not where you are concerned."

"I — couldn't bear for you to hate me."

"No," I pressed her fingers to my lips, holding desperately with that simple touch. "No, I could never hate you. I will always cherish what I do have with you... always."

"Whether it be years or months?"

I nodded, holding her gaze.

She looked away then, at the leather binding of sketches in her lap. "I expect I should finish the roughs for you this week." She smiled suddenly — tender in reassuring me now. "I don't expect anything will happen before spring, but... I'd hate to leave you without something to work with over the winter."

I smiled in return. This was her book — her ideas blossoming into a storyboard book. My text was the supporting role this time, and it would be her drawings which told of the little cloud that swirled and shaped and searched — through elephants and cats and quail — for something to be, only to discover that a cloud was the best thing for a cloud to be.

"The lady does, because the lady is," I murmured, warm beneath the rekindled hope and spirit of her eyes. "It's going to be the best book we've done, you know."

"Maybe...," she considered that for a second. "It's a little like a family book of our own, isn't it?"

"How do you mean?"

"For Jake and Grandmama, for the both of us. They've been steady, caring people throughout our lives — despite...." She blushed.

"Our love?" I supplied, knowing she still wrestled so often against any labeling words.

Her expression grew more curious then. "I've never quite understood your Uncle Jake. How — calm he is, always taking everything in stride. I don't—" she shrugged helplessly, "I don't really have a reference for him. He's so very different from Dickie — from so many of the men I know.

"Dear Heavens," she laughed at the sudden thought, "can you see Dickie, if he found out about the two of us?"

"I'd rather not dwell on it," I grimaced.

"But Jake," her eyes were clear as they met mine, "he does know, doesn't he?"

I nodded, feeling the fondness I held for him rise inside. "It's not something he'd ever talk about directly. He'd say, he's not one for prying. But it's... well, it's his way of showing respect."

"It's a way Dickie would never understand."

"Jake is older," I reminded her gently, full well knowing that she would always regret not being closer to her brother in some way.

"Age doesn't always breed tolerance, Wren... let alone acceptance."

"True, it doesn't."

"Yet Jake wants so very badly to see you happy?"

I nodded. "I think that's why, whatever I choose to do — if it's because I'm being true to me, he'll accept it... he'll accept me. He saw my world fall apart when I was nine and ten, Annabel. He saw my father forget my birthdays, he saw my desperateness for independence — because even then I knew the paper shell I would become, if I blindly followed my father's plans of convenience. Jake saw me hurt so badly that there is no place for him to compromise now. Nothing short of my happiness... he wants to see that, and he will support anything that may yield it — whether I follow convention or not. He's seen what convention might do to me, and I don't think he liked it. It's just that simple."

"No," Annabel shook her head, "it's not simple. It's never simple for people to live by their convictions, to balance the integrity and the compromise."

"We acknowledge who we are and what must be," I amended quietly, reminding her of us — of Grandmama — of loyalties binding. "And then we choose best how to live with ourselves."

* * *

That winter it was my turn to leave Annabel a Christmas token with Mrs. Hodges. It was a silver ring, on a silver chain, with the same creeping rose vines etched into it that her jewelry box and locket held. But this time, the inscription inside the band read Beloved — and next to it was a heart.

The Eleventh Summer
Chapter Seventeen

It was May and the waters were a steely gray color, promising rougher weather for the night. The air smelled of rain in the chilly, damp way that is reminiscent of heavy mists and steady downpours. The sky above was just a foreboding with its lines of black where the gray clouds had grown so dense. Spring was not so old a season yet, and the winter edge to the weather was still there.

The breeze was cold and tousled my hair, chilling my ears as my nose grew pink. My shoulders hunched, shrugging my sheepskin coat high to guard my neck. But it was not a complaining gesture. This again was the sort of weather my lake offered all too frequently, and it stirred my blood and teased my soul. It was weather that made me feel alive. After a winter of ice encased stillness, the restless waters and shivering leaves were welcomed.

It was spring, and as drenched as that meant I was apt to get, it was marvelous. And — it was that much closer to summer.

The thought of Annabel's return in mid-June had awakened with the budding new maple leaves. It was growing stronger with each day, the waiting pensive and yet so much a natural part of my life now that it seemed less a burden and more a kindred sort of season spirit. It was the thing that swung me out across the lake with a slow, leisurely run to pass by the dilapidated old dock whenever I went way south for bait or motor supplies.

Or rather, whenever I returned with such supplies... like this evening. The battered, hulking shell of the Standish summer house and I had become familiar friends of a sort. But I knew that with the mists folding in, I wouldn't even be able to see her weary frame tonight.

I suppose it didn't much matter, but I spun the wheel 'round a bit, still following the shoreline. I was in no hurry to deliver the bulky engine. Paul wouldn't be puttering with the motor until morning, the wind wasn't threatening anything my weather worn boat couldn't handle, and I was — I admitted — enjoying myself.

I followed the shore as the bay opened up, my boat put-putting along with a deep-throated rumble.

The weeping willows drooped like wet, dangling mops in the mistiness, and the worn platform of the dock emerged from the mire. Movement and a clunk caught my attention, and I cut the motor back, peering forward as a light — no a second one, suddenly flickered into being. It lifted high, and I knew that the lanterns had been hung on the dock ends to ward off drifting boats.

To ward off? Or to beckon?

Distant footsteps rang as a dim figure, clad in long skirts, began to make its way back down the dock.

My heart stopped, and my hand shook as it pushed the throttle down a bit.

The engine roared to life. The figure stopped, still not to shore.

I felt my breath catch with concern. That it was Annabel was not questioned by me... that she was here so soon brought alarm and foreboding.

She stood unmoving as I killed the motor, drifting in the last few feet to bump the deck and grab the slender dock posts. She stood unmoving as I leapt out to tie the lines and, finally, as I turned to her.

We stood there, I in my damp sheepskin... she in her heavy shawl. We were merely a few feet apart. Yet in the hand-span of a breath, the endless years of our times seemingly suspended us.

Then there was a sob cutting through the fog and my name in the midst of the cry. My arms opened and pulled Annabel near, wrapping tightly around her shaking frame. And I realized these tears had been there even as I had watched her light the lanterns.

"It's all right now," I whispered, stroking her hair and shoulders — holding her with all the tender strength I could muster. "It's all right now. I'm here... we'll make it all right."

I feared she would grow sick as the choking sobs racked through her body.

I noticed then that her hair was down. Her dress hung loosely, and beneath the grasp of my hands I felt her ribs, not the ivory bones of a corset. An utter fearfulness grew within me, and I pushed her from me, shaking her faintly to snatch her attention.

"What's wrong?" and my words were distinct, my voice demanding. "Has somebody hurt you?!"

Her eyes were wide, stricken as she choked back a gasp and managed a shake of her head.

"Thank God!" My heart started again and I grasped her close once more, cradling her head to my chest. "I'm sorry... for one moment I thought.... What's wrong, Love? Can you tell me?"

She was better now, gathering herself together some. The tears were turning to sniffles. But her fingers clung to the fleece of my coat, and I tightened my clasp.

"I'm here," I murmured, kissing her hair tenderly. "I'm here."

She nodded, finding the strength to straighten and search for her handkerchief, but my hands were gentle as they stayed to her shoulders.

"Annabel—?"

"It's Grandmama," she mumbled behind her kerchief. She drew a ragged breath and forced herself to look at me. "She's been ill most of the year. Doctors call it a small sort of stroke and—" her face crumpled but she grit her teeth and fought, finding her voice at last to say, "—she's dying Wren."

I held her, my face wet with my own tears.

"It's been so hard — watching her grow stronger bit by bit, only to have it taken away from her again."

A little corner of my mind recognized how much she needed me right now, and I pushed aside my own grief for later. "I'm here, Love—"

"Oh—!" she pressed — collapsed into me as if drawing strength from our very contact, and it seemed some of the trembling eased, "so much has changed."

"I'm here...."

She nodded, standing taller with eyes still shut. "I'm so glad you are."

"I am."

"You knew to come? We're so early. It's not even summer season...?" Her eyes were pleading then, almost beginning to doubt me as her hands curled about my arms. "How — ? Why did you—?"

"I just did."

She accepted that, knowing there really was no other answer. Her head bent and her murmur was barely to be heard, "Can you stay the night?"

"Yes—" I cupped her face in my hands, tipping her up to look at me again, and repeated, "yes."

She shuddered, eyes closing and hands covering mine.

Very, very gently I kissed her.

Her arms wrapped around my neck, and she hugged me fiercely, her lips finding my ear, "I love you!"

"I love you."

Her expression was grateful as she released me, and I turned reluctantly to tend to the boat.

In the gathering gloom of twilight, I called Jake on the short wave and told him what was happening. The static-thick channel brought a distorted voice back but his sympathy was not to be masked. And he stepped in as any good partner to pick-up the slack as I needed him.

"Wren, Honey, Paul needs that motor come morning or the weekend's Rockman party is going to need canceling. Should I come fetch it from you? Over."

I paused in quick thought, then shook my head as I answered, "No. I'll bring it by early-ish. I need to get some clothes and things — I don't know how long I'll be needed here. Over."

"Let it take as long as it needs, Jenny. We'll manage. Give them our regards, girl. We'll be praying. Over."

I glanced at Annabel, and she nodded with a watery smile. She'd heard.

"Consider it done. And Jake — thanks."

"No call for it. Out."

The house seemed unusually quiet and yet it was filled with people. But Mrs. Hodges had grown taciturn in her grief and seemed capable of only uttering orders to her staff. A closed-faced, kind of pain pulled at the corners of her mouth now as she nodded courteously to me; although to be fair, she had so many more people to manage. The whole atmosphere had retained the formality of their Philadelphia residence. It seemed the footman, the upstairs maid, the cook and Grandmama's nurse had all accompanied them this year. Still, they almost seemed to be intruders; and somewhat grimly I watched as Annabel ordered the parlor doors closed, leaving word not to be disturbed unless Grandmama called.

Annabel's competence and authority were obviously respected by all the staff. The footman in his gray waistcoat bowed politely enough as he left the tea tray, and the doors slid silently into place behind him. But the toll of hiding her concern for Grandmama was plain to me, even as I understood. She was responsible for the livelihood and security of these people just as I was for those Jake and I employed. She was not allowed the luxury of collapse here — they needed her show of strength just as she now needed their able assistance in caring for her grandmother.

Her hair was bound tidily back into place, a soft knot upon her head, and her heavy shawl had been replaced with a more delicate one, its silken pattern matching the deep blue of her plain dress — she no longer looked like the small, frightened waif who had stood so silently as I fastened the canvas on my boat. But I noticed the whiteness of her knuckles as she gripped the teapot. And I noticed the deliberate calm of her movements as she measured sugar and passed me a cup.

There was a price she was paying for this outward appearance.

"When did she fall sick?" I asked quietly, very aware of how little Annabel had touched me when handing me the tea.

"Last November." She cleared her throat and

folded her hand neatly in her lap. Her own tea was forgotten. "It happened during the night apparently. I suspect, there may have been earlier attacks, but — she has never said."

"Why do you think there were others?"

"Subtle changes? She began taking very good care of herself — almost fanatically. We began to decline evening invitations. Our own entertainment became limited to the odd brunch or afternoon tea. It wasn't like her to consistently forego seances and society gatherings, especially with the century turning. But it seemed as if all the predictions and alluring suppositions had simply lost their appeal. And then—"

She paused, composing herself to go on. "Christmas was very quiet. She was completely bedridden — found it difficult to speak even. And Dickie descended all set to take charge of the situation — close the house, move us to New York for better watching until... until it could be arranged that Edward and I marry. Then Grandmama — of course — would be welcomed to spend the last of her days in the house at Boston."

I frowned into my tea at the bitterness in her voice. I usually thought of Dickie as shallow and terribly inconsiderate, but I had underestimated him. He was a soulless gutter rat!

"I wanted to thank you for the ring," she said suddenly, her hand touching her heart, and I realized she must be wearing it on its chain beneath her dress. "It was very much needed when received. It gave me the resolve to stand up to him — to counter his orders with staff. And I sought out her physicians to reiterate the risks of travel or any forced changes at so late a date."

An amused, ironic sort of look touched her,

"Edward unexpectedly came to my rescue as well. I realize he had no love for the idea of taking on a reluctant wife and an elderly invalid. But his selfishness worked to my advantage this time. He sided with the doctors. So—" she laughed without much humor, "he believes he is being quite gallant and winning my everlasting gratitude as he patiently waits for my service to Grandmama to end. Then — he will whisk me off to his grand, gray stone estate to console me in my grief."

The china cup and saucer suddenly felt very fragile in my hands; rage took me, burning into my soul. Carefully I set the tea aside and flexed my fingers, willing patience to return.

"Then, things began to change again. She began to recover, always though, feigning more strength for Dickie's visits until—" Annabel set her mouth firmly. "Grandmama said she'd be damned to hell and beyond before she'd see either of us taken from Philadelphia. She went into a fury last time Dickie suggested a moving to New York. The next day she was stricken again. I don't know if it was from her anger, or if perhaps she sensed it to come and grew so vehement in an attempt to prevent Dickie's next plan. But Dickie took it as an indication that she was no longer in her right mind, and in April, upon his return to New York, he sought out the family solicitors.

"All that we own, Wren, is in trust under Grandmama's executives' control, until such time as she deems Dickie ready to take over the responsibilities. It has always been a tacit understanding that Papa meant her to tend to household and goods until she died and that Dickie would acquire the control of the business as the executives saw fit — which has been the way of it for years."

"What of you?" I asked warily.

Annabel was silent a moment, then, "There are no specific provisions for me. I was not yet born when Papa wrote out the agreements. It was just after his own father had died, you see. Later, it was simply assumed I'd be provided for by Dickie, until such time as I married or—"

"Or until you become an unappealing spinster to be politely closeted off?"

She pursed her lips, almost smiling as she remembered her own description of her plans to avoid Edward. "Yes."

"Then, Dickie is protesting the conditions of the will now, on the grounds that Grandmama is mentally incompetent?"

"Mentally and physically," Annabel nodded quickly. "If he succeeds, he will ask Edward to 'rescue' me earlier. He has already explained to me how unhealthy it is to be exposed to Grandmama's insensible ravings and how he fears some irreparable emotional damage to me—"

"And Grandmama?"

"He graciously assures me, he will employ the best nurses and physicians, engage a local barrister to monitor the funds and leave her nicely ensconced in the Philadelphia house. Visitors will be limited and supervised — to a 'select' few friends. It seems, he intends to create a 'soothing' environment for her."

That civility and hypocrisy would kill her more quickly than a New England winter, I thought sourly.

But as Annabel's gaze fell to the fire, I pulled myself back from my bitterness. The edges of her mouth were white from the tense press of her lips.... Her hands were clenched with her nails cutting into her palms.

With a muffled curse, I slid down the sofa and gathered her into my arms.

"Damn the servants," I muttered as she stiffened, and after a brief breath of indecision she slumped back into me with such relief that I thought I would cry.

"Would you sleep with me tonight...?"

My arms tightened at her whispered request, "Of course I will."

"I don't think... Mrs. Hodges just assumes we do. I mean, we always have since we were so little and—"

"Hush," I spoke to her fears, "you need me. Nothing will take me away tonight."

"Oh Wren—" Her arms covered mine as I rocked her gently. And I felt her control slipping with a choked sob, "I'm so frightened."

"Shhh—" I buried my lips in her hair. "You're going to make yourself sick like this. Now take a deep breath—"

She obeyed, and wearily her head tipped back to my shoulder. I brushed her cheek with a tender kiss.

"Can you tell me the rest of it? Or should we leave it until morning?"

"There's little more to say." Her head moved in neither a nod nor a shake, and her words carried her fatigue in their hollowness. "Grandmama has been determined to return to this house since her first attack. Naturally Dickie objected — my dilemma has been in advocating summer travel and yet protesting a transition to New York.

"Then about two weeks ago, he wrote to Mrs. Hodges — in confidence — saying he would be arriving in Philadelphia and please be advised to ready his quarters as well as a suite for Cousin Edward. I think Dickie underestimated their bond, because Mrs. Hodges has been with Grandmama too long to keep such news to herself.

"So Grandmama asked me to arrange an immediate departure.

"She was insistent, Wren — she kept repeating she must see you about sealed letters." Annabel's puzzled gaze turned to me, "Do you know what she's meaning?"

I frowned, until I remembered the ribbon-tied envelopes Mr. Thomas had presented to me so long ago. "Maybe... yes. When she gave me the jewelry, she also gave me some things to be read at a later date. She had asked, I promise not to open the envelopes until she explained them to me — someday."

"Then you can get them? Bring them back with you tomorrow?"

With a nod, "Of course."

"I was so worried Dickie might finally have been right. I couldn't think what she meant."

"And what of Dickie's arrival in Philadelphia?"

This time it was her turn to frown. "He'll find us gone and follow here. I'm sure of it. He knows her plans have been focused on this house — on this summer's trip. And Grandmama's coachman will not lie to him if questioned directly."

"When will he be here then?"

"Day after tomorrow, I think. He'll come in on the late morning train if he can get tickets. Early evening, if he's delayed... and Edward will be with him."

My determination set with a steely anger beneath it. "Then your loving brother shall have me to deal with as well."

She touched my face lightly, her eyes clear in their appeal. "Thank you."

Chapter Eighteen

I lay awake for most of the night, my mind churning with the implications of all which had been said. Again and again I returned to but one solution, yet my resolve wavered in voicing it. There was no way in even knowing if it was possible, and I grimly decided things had gone too long unsaid. If Grandmama was going to see me, then there were things of my own to be asked as well.

Annabel slept utterly exhausted through the long hours of my musings, flinching from dark nightmares as she lay, curled around my encircling arm with her back against me. I had thought to hold her briefly before readying myself for bed and had kicked off my shoes, sitting on the quilt beside her to stroke her back quietly as the tears had come again. But when she drifted to sleep, I'd found myself loath to release her as she clung to me. Finally, I had settled myself against the headboard to address my own upended emotions.

How Dickie could treat his own sister as some sort of irritating object to be promptly dispensed with I did not know... nor understand. At this point, I had no desire to even try to grasp his self-perceived dilemmas. The only point I kept coming back to was his long battle of wits against his sister's wishes not to marry... that long assumed role of his to control her life. With an intensely jealous hatred, I despised the very fact he had any rights to control her at all. Though if I had any say in the matter, it was a fact that was going to change and soon.

A brisk knock at the door shook me from my ruminations. From her lack of servant's garb I recognized Grandmama's nurse, Mrs. King, as she pushed in through the door. Her astonishment caught her in mid-step, and I gave the woman a long, measuring stare.

It was a bluff. Inside my heart was suddenly racing, and I was surprisingly very thankful that I was fully dressed with my legs stretched out on top of the quilt. Now was not the time for confrontations with strangers; we couldn't afford the luxury of battling homophobic enemies with Dickie on the way. Yet as Mrs. King's gaze fell to Annabel's sleeping form, her mouth closed with a tender sort of smile.

The muscles in the small of my back relaxed in gratitude. Annabel obviously had been winning the loyalty of more than just the long employed, regular staff.

With a softer tread and the skirts of her gray dress held to keep them from rustling, Mrs. King approached as quietly as she could. She leaned near and whispered, "The Grandmama Standish has asked for Miss Cassel again."

"I'm Jennifer Cassel." I answered her in the same soft tone. "I'll be right along—"

She shook her head, putting up a hand to forestall my movement. "The Grandmama Standish already sleeps again, Miss. And it will do Miss Annabel good to have more herself. My but I must say! It is a relief to finally meet you. I was beginning to harbor a few doubts. I'm Mrs. King—"

"I'd thought so," I smiled in return. "I've heard good things of you. It's a pleasure to meet you."

She nodded towards Annabel, "Has she been sleeping long?"

"Since about midnight. So what—? About six hours?"

"Good Lord of Mercy," Mrs. King shook her head in amazement. "I haven't seen her sleep on through the night since my Christmas arrival. And in these last three weeks, she's had barely nothing but a catnap or two."

I felt that grim hatred for Dickie grip me again.

"The Grandmama Standish—" Mrs. King brought me back to the reason of her intrusion, "she would like to speak with you sometime today. Is that possible? She's been quite distressed about reaching you."

"I'll be here. There are a few errands I must run, but I'll be back by early afternoon and I'll bring the papers she wants."

Mrs. King let out a breath of relief. "I want to thank you so, Miss Cassel. I'll be sure to tell Herself when she wakes. It will mean a great deal to her, I assure you."

"She means a great deal to me," I murmured, but Mrs. King was already quietly departing across the carpet.

The door clicked shut very softly, and Annabel moved, luxuriating in a slow stretch of stiffened legs as she rolled back into my body. Without opening an eye, she mumbled sleepily, "Is she gone?"

I chuckled, a low happy sound from the sudden warmth stirring in my heart. There was a piece to my beloved Annabel that was absolutely incorrigible.

"Yes, she's gone."

Annabel gave voice to something caught between a pleased purr and a reluctant groan. Then with a flop, she was once again on top of my arm, holding tightly.

"I don't want to get up."

"You don't have to," I reassured her indulgently.

"That was Mrs. King?" Her sleepy tone surfaced again.

"Yes."

"Is Grandmama all right?"

"Yes," I whispered, leaning over her with a smile. "Now go back to sleep."

"Hmmm...."

I laughed low and soft, pressing a kiss to her shoulder. But her grasp tightened on my one arm as I went to move away.

"You're leaving?"

"Not 'til seven — seven-thirty. Then I'll be back by lunch."

"What time is it now?"

"Around six."

"Ohh...."

"Shh, you've time to sleep."

A small, warm hand slipped into mine, fingers stretching and then intertwining with my own. "Soft...."

"Nice... now sleep!"

"I don't want to...." Her fingers began to stroke a sensitive place on my wrist. "But I'm still half asleep."

"That's a nice place to be," I murmured, gently tucking the hair behind her ear. "Just drift for a while, I'm here—"

"Uhm-umm!" and there was the sound of a petulant child in that. "I don't want to."

I smiled, my pulse quickening even as I felt a protective tenderness swell within me. "What do you want, Love?"

"Uhm–hmmm...."

"Hmm?"

"Couldn't you put a chair in front of the door or something? The one at the desk jams beneath the doorknobs nicely."

"Oh, does it?"

"Haven't you missed me...?" That woe-be-gone little minx voice was back.

"Yes — I have missed you," and with warm breath and moist tongue I captured her ear.

She gasped and arched back into me. I could feel the length of her pressed against me even through the blankets.

"Wren...?"

"I'll get the door."

* * *

Coat in hand, I pushed myself away from the wall as the door opened and Annabel emerged from Grandmama's room. Over her shoulder I caught a glimpse of the great canopied bed and the small, still figure it housed. Then the door was closing and Annabel was sighing, almost as if she'd been holding her breath in her quiet crossing of that room.

"How is she?"

"I wish I knew." Annabel shrugged, shaking her head with bewilderment and pain. "She sleeps with such exhaustion, but I don't know if it's from the trip or another attack... or perhaps even from relief at finally being here."

That would have to satisfy me. I drew Annabel near for a quick hug, kissing her forehead even as my gaze remained fixed to Grandmama's door.

Her hand patted my chest, and she stepped back, "Everything's done that may be, for the moment, Wren. Worrying doesn't help."

I smiled, the familiar reins of practicality were once again in her hands. I straightened a fold in the square lace yoke of her blouse and nodded, "You're right, as always."

She gave me a wry little smile and pushed her hands into her skirt pockets. "I've made you late enough as it is."

"It's all right. Walk me down to the boat?"

She hesitated and then declined with regret, "I need to see to the staff. And I should stay close for Grandmama."

"I understand," I leaned near for a gentle kiss, wondering at the softness that could offer such reassurance and yet still make me flutter in my stomach.

"You'll be back for lunch?"

"Or just after. Don't wait on me. I'll grab a sandwich from the lodge if I need to."

Chapter Nineteen

The sun was warm and the lake a gentle lapping of gray-blue. It was a beautiful, calm spring day, with the coolness of the waters chilling the metal hull of the canoe beneath my knees. The breeze smelled fresh and clean, almost catching the scent of that last melted snow of April past. The dip and swell of my paddle blended with the peace of the day, and I felt the melancholy lose a little of its despair.

I drew up to shore, gliding down the dock's long length. The quiet of the trip across had done me good, and I found myself glad I'd elected to leave the motorboat. My decision had been seemingly based on business sense — I hadn't known how long I would be gone and so I hadn't wanted to tie up a fishing boat. But the long, silent trip across had settled my jitters and helpless feelings. My role was not yet clearly defined here, and patience was more suited to my needs than anger now — patience for waiting, such a small thing that took so much strength. At least now, I felt I had some to offer her.

The house still felt strange as I mounted the steps, knapsack in hand, and I remembered it was filled with so many strangers. I knocked, wistfully regretful that I could no longer merely walk in.

"Yes Miss?"

"It's all right, Gerard. You can go."

The footman declined his head in a polite bow, fading away as Annabel appeared at the screen door. But she didn't invite me in, instead she joined me on the porch. I followed as she moved down the railing away from the open doors and passing servants.

"Grandmama is awake," she murmured, her back to me as she stood gazing down that endless lawn. "We talked, despite her weariness... she felt it important."

"Is she all right?" I set my things down on a wicker chair.

"Yes, well — she's no worse." Annabel shrugged uncomfortably. "She — she has quite a lot to tell you. Wren...?"

I started towards her but she moved away quickly, so I stopped.

Her back was ramrod straight. Her hands danced nervously along the verandah's railing. If it hadn't been for those hands, she would have looked every inch the poised, young lady of the house. But I was confused, because I knew that — at least for the moment — she was not.

"What Grandmama said worries you," I noted warily. "Should I know something before...?"

"It's hers to tell." Annabel turned around to me, attempting to meet my gaze and failing.

"Then we'll talk after I see her," I asserted gently.

"Yes, I think we must." She swallowed hard and finally managed to face me, eyes beseeching. "I didn't know, Wren. You must believe me? I didn't know."

"Of course I believe you."

Grandmama had changed much more than I had imagined... much more than I could have ever prepared myself for. The stately persona, the silver coiled hair... the quick smile that lit her humor and chased the sternness from her countenance... all was gone. In her place I found a fragile, old woman with skin so thin, her bones stretched it white as she clasped my hand in hers... with wrists so bruised from the sheer weight of her nightgown, they were black and purple. Her grasp trembled. Her right hand was barely able to close about my own, while her left lay almost helpless in her lap.

The shawl, her favorite of indigo blues, was wrapped about her — almost dwarfing her pale figure with its color and bulk — as she sat there, propped high. Her hair tumbled about her shoulders, a dull, thin pewter in shade. She looked lost among the coverlet and plumped pillows which supported her, and it seemed to take all her strength to turn her head towards me as I gently settled on the bedside.

Mrs. King left us quietly, reminding me to ring the bell on the night stand should we need anything.

I felt my throat close in pity and in fear. I was so afraid of hurting this poor woman beside me, even from the mere touch of my hand. But her eyes, gray as a winter's storm, were alert and followed my expression — my emotions with little difficulty.

"Yes, I have changed, my child," and her voice, although hoarse, was surprisingly strong. Again she registered my surprise, and her eyes crinkled a little at the corners as her mouth struggled with a tired smile. "No, it is the old shell that is withering, dear Jennifer. The mind is still quite capable, whatever it be worth."

I covered her hand so that I cradled it with both of mine and with an effort blinked back the tears. "I'm going to miss you, Grandmama."

She grunted with satisfaction, almost tightening her clasp for an instant. "At least you speak directly. Of the lot of them, only Annabel and yourself ever bother with the truth of it."

"Well," I managed gallantly, "tact has never been my strong suit, has it?"

"On the contrary," she breathed wearily, "you always held your tongue when you needed to. You're a good woman, Jennifer... a fine young person you've grown to be. I like to think, perhaps, I have had a little to do with that — but then again perhaps not. Sometimes the stars tend to decide these things themselves."

"No," I assured her, "you've had some say. You and the vegetable gardens."

She laughed weakly at our old jest of threatened discipline.

I smiled and settled a little more comfortably onto the bed. Suddenly, I was very glad to have this chance to see her again.

"Enough of past folly." Grandmama's eyes grew wide with the intensity of her need. "Did you bring them, Jennifer?"

"Yes," and I moved gingerly to pull the envelopes from the back pocket of my blue jeans.

"Not yet," her hand fluttered, resting finally on top of the crumpled, knotted ribbon. "First, the beginning...."

I nodded and picked up her hand again.

"When my husband died, you know I began my search for the gates to beyond...?"

I nodded again, supplying, "Annabel has always told me, your love for seances and the occult stems from that time."

"Yes, and then grew from what I began to learn about myself — about the spirit."

"Have you reached him then? Your husband?"

Her eyes closed briefly. "I will see him soon enough, child." She returned to me then. "There are a great many things to be learned from places other than here — and from times other than now,

Jennifer."

I swallowed uncomfortably.

"You are aware of the time differences, child. I know... and remember the questions I would not answer for you. And I have watched you with Annabel since. You have both grown, adapting to and yet struggling with the mysteries which bring you together even as they separate your lives. You do know of the difference—"

"Yes," my mouth grew dry, "we are of different times."

"And you have done well to adapt — to question so seldom."

"I — we came to conclude... somehow it was your own doing."

"My clever children." The faintest of nods moved her as her eyes sparkled with pride. "Have you pondered too on the magic of how?"

"Literal magic?" I shook my head slowly in confusion. "As in the seances?"

"Ahh no, a more powerful sort... the believing sort." An incredibly gentle smile of serenity took Grandmama Standish, and the wheezing left her breath. "The difference between make-believe and magic, dear Jennifer, is simply in the believing."

I considered that in silence, but I could find no argument... nor any need to construct one. Grandmama was here, holding my hand. Annabel was below on the verandah. Across the lake, Jake and Mrs. Stevens waited with their unconditional acceptance and loving comfort. Paul struggled with motor parts, mutely wishing strength to both Annabel and I. Quite simply, my life had always embraced 'an era of yesterday' meshing with my here-and-now — just as Annabel's included 'a time of tomorrows.' So I found, I could not question this "magic" of Grandmama's. To do so, would mean to refute Annabel's presence in my life… in my heart.

Again I looked to Grandmama. "Must I learn this magic then? Or at least — why you've done this?"

"Yes, some of the why you must understand. On that first day — it was during a fine spring day, not unlike this one, perhaps? I was in Philadelphia. I'd been meditating, waiting for my guests to gather for an evening séance… when I awoke to find myself beside M'dam Randolph."

"M'dam Randolph of Lily Dale?"

"The very same. She was in her home, with a young visitor. They were reading the cards.

"I was struck by the visiting girl's likeness to my own self in my youth. Her hair was perhaps golder, her dress entirely too untidy for my tastes — but nevertheless, she was a child of my own family, I'd thought. And then, M'dam Randolph was struck by my presence, and the mystery to unfold.

"The child… oh, really not such a child, she was in her twenties… was my great-grandchild. The date was not my own, you see. She told me this most remarkable story then, about my lovely Annabel and poor Richard.

"She was Richard's orphan. It seemed… well, she told me of all that was to come and of my own role in the matter."

"I thought…," Grandmama's eyes slid shut with the faintness of her sigh. "I thought myself quite mad for weeks afterward. But I consulted and listened and found this thing less and less strange. You see, there had been such a familiar way to this child, I could not help but believe her."

She looked weary now as Grandmama brought

a dulled gaze back to me. "I looked more carefully at Richard then. Already a boy of eleven — half-formed man that he was, I saw more clearly than before. I saw his stubbornness as less childishness and more as selfishness. I saw his teasing was designed to undermine his sister's opinions — a way to make her concede to his arguments. Perhaps he had gone too long neglected his father? Or simply, too long spoiled — pandered too as the little man of the house by myself? I don't know—"

I patted her hand encouragingly, reminding her of her earlier words, "Or perhaps the stars merely meant it to be?"

She sent me a look of gratitude and drew a breath to continue. "I began to address Annabel's needs more thoroughly. I asserted her right to choices and opinions and sought the broadest range of tutors imaginable for her education. I knew, Jennifer, that she must be prepared — capable of accepting the most outlandish of ideas if your world was not to seem forebodingly alien to her. And I sought my colleagues again, to find the elusive doorway back to this place and time. M'dam Randolph is a crucial focus for many things in this era, and we were simpatico — attuned to the same nuances of stars and spirits — until finally the door reopened, to an earlier place in her life's scheme and M'dam received my pleas with an open heart."

"So together, you then created this summer haven for Annabel."

"Haven? Yes." Her fingers sought the envelopes. "Open them?"

Again that faintest of nods, "It is time."

Outwardly I was efficient as I pulled apart the blue ribbons and broke the wax seals. But my heart pounded almost painfully, and I wondered why I wasn't shaking uncontrollably.

"Birth certificates?" I did not recognize the first Standish name, but the second document was made out for Annabel. "Nineteen-sixty—?"

"Annabel was to have her choice, Jennifer." For a brief moment, the echo of an older authority rose in Grandmama's voice. "She is to have her choice."

I blinked, slow in my confusion.

"I have always known what Richard believes he is duty-bound to do for family and firm. I grew more and more to dread his iron-selfish hand, and the toll it will exact from Annabel.

"I have taught her not to marry unless she chooses, Jennifer. But the alternative has never been to stay here — where Richard's will can reach and bend her destiny.

"You — you are her choice... her alternative. If she declines marriage to Edward, then she must claim a place in your life — in your time. Mr. Thomas arranged the certificates to allow this...."

She waited, unable to tell what I was thinking. And indeed, I was too stunned to be 'thinking' anything except — Annabel might be able to stay with me? Was it truly possible?

"There is more. The woman who will marry Edward, should Annabel decline, will defy convention as well. It seems, the poor fellow is destined for an enlightening marriage whether he wills it or not — " The joke died quickly on her lips. "She too will follow the stars and the spirits... she too will become acquainted with M'dam Randolph, if only briefly. And so when Richard and his wife die, their surviving child will come to join Annabel... if you will have her." Grandmama paused, weighing her words carefully before, "Jennifer, I could not spare Annabel from the harshness of losing her own parents — I know better than to think Richard would believe any warning I could utter about his sea voyage."

"He will drown too?" I interrupted suddenly, remembering his parents' fate.

"He and his wife in 1912. They will be on a ship that strays from course and sinks from carelessness."

It didn't seem fair — even for Dickie.

"I can not save him, but I dare to hope I may spare Annabel... and my dear great-grandchild... from the wars and depression which fill the first half of your century."

Stunned, I looked at Grandmama. Never had she hinted at knowledge beyond her own years of living.

A dry, humorless chuckle stirred in her at my astonishment. "I have walked through many places one should never need walk, my child. There is wisdom beyond knowledge, horrors beyond aging that my time-out-of-time has shown me. My sorrow is in my helplessness, not in my intentions."

And then, "So speak, Jennifer Cassel, will you take Annabel beyond her brother's tauntings? Will you take her — and my great-grandchild to safety? Do you love her enough?"

"Yes, she may come — they both may come with me," I rasped, catching Grandmama's hand in desperation. "Can you truly send her to stay here — in this time of mine? Is it possible?"

"It has been your destiny to accept in this possibility," Grandmama's smile began to wane, her head sinking deeply into the pillows about her. "I knew of you before that afternoon when young Jennifer Cassel swam into our beach. Yes, my child, if you will take Annabel — if you will fade into the misty waters with her beside you. But it must be soon."

"Soon? How soon?" Her eyes closed and I grew alarmed, "Grandmama! Please, I must know?"

A sigh, labored with fatigue drew her back. Her hand moved weakly in mine. "I am no fool, Jennifer. Richard comes. My strength leaves. I will not see this spring's end. Neither of you nor Annabel should face Richard — nor rely on me to hold strong beneath his vexation. It all grows too much. You must leave, if you are to leave... in the morning before his arrival. And he will arrive on the early train.

"You must take her to your lodge — into your sweet haven of 'tomorrow' and hold her beside you, Jennifer. Use the jewels I sent to find her money when — if her sketches do not. Or if there is a need, when the toddler arrives in the next years. If Annabel so chooses, please... take her beyond her brother — beyond the scattered savages of this first half century."

"Yes," I swore, pressing a kiss to that trembling hand I held. "I will see it done — for you, for her... for all of us."

"There is a last thing."

"What?"

"I have not spoken to Annabel of young Lucy — nor of Richard's death. Promise me, you will hold your tongue in this for now. Her decision will be difficult enough as it is. If she believes she might spare him by staying and persuading him from the trip later—?"

"I understand." I sighed, admitting I did not like this condition, but selfishly I would keep this one last trust in spite of my conscience. "I will do as you ask."

A sigh escaped her and I recognized the end of the weary journey this woman had made. She'd spent a lifetime in carving a future for her granddaughter —

a lifetime of struggle in abandoning her grandson. I would not have chosen her place for anything. But I was grateful she had done as she had.

Gently, I placed a kiss to her forehead as she slipped into slumber. Her part was nearly done. The rest was left to me now... and to Annabel.

Chapter Twenty

I let the screen door close carefully and stood for a moment as I looked at Annabel. She was half-perched on the railing, watching the play of sunlight and shadows in the thicket along side of the house. Her back was against one of the porch posts, and she did not turn at the sound of the door.

With a grim smile I noticed she'd laid the verandah table with afternoon tea. It didn't matter, the hour was too early — the gesture was one of normalcy in a situation that seemed anything but normal.

"She's sleeping now," I offered quietly.

"Is she?"

I saw Annabel hastily wipe the tears from her cheeks. She was careful to keep her back to me.

"Would you like some tea?" she amended.

"No thank you."

She continued staring out into the afternoon sunshine.

"I want to talk, Annabel."

She nodded, and I heard a ragged breath drawn. "It's not very fair, is it Wren?"

"No," I agreed slowly, "I'll miss her too."

"I don't mean—!" She bit off her words harshly, rising to pace further away. She hesitated, curling her fists in a helpless, useless kind of gesture as frustration gripped her. She risked a glance at me and spun to grab the railing in anger. "It's not fair to you!"

I shifted, leaning against the door with my hands in my back pockets. Then I waited.

"She talks about choices." Annabel half-turned to me, "All our lives she's talked about choices. About being who I am and not bending to convention — or convenience! She's taught me about honesty to myself, in what I want, what I need — in the compromises I choose or choose not to make. In everything!

"And yet—? All this time, she's been planning — manipulating you into this!

"She's put you in a position, Wren, where you have to do what she says or see me tied to Dickie's precious Edward! And I don't see where any of this is respecting your place in her grand schemes!" Her voice caught with a sob as she looked away. "Where is the honesty in manipulating you for eleven years? Where is your right of choice—?"

She was crying now, no longer hiding it from herself or from me. "Where is your life left to be even your own?!"

I dropped my head, wondering if there was a way to find words for this — words that she could believe in... words that she could dare to trust.

A pebble moved beneath the toe of my shoe. I pushed it through a crack in the boards as a short sigh gathered in me.

"My life?" I looked up past the lawns and the trees to the lake I knew lay hidden out there... and I felt the words come. "My life is made of only summers, Annabel. When the fall comes, I am torn — bloodied! — by a cruelty that slashes deep it severs my very heart from my soul.

"I search for some sense of resignation — for acceptance of the inevitable.... For patience? But the autumn ifsfilled with burnished golds and bronzed reds in its leaves which only remind me of your hair in the sunlight, in the firelight... in candlelight? And I find no solace, until winter finally comes with its coldness to wrap its icy fingers around my feelings and I grow numb — grow grateful! Because the pain ebbs.

Except the stars above are so clear on those crisp nights. And yet I keep wondering at these shadows my eye glimpse, knowing it can't be yet hoping it will be you. But of course, it never is. So I try to fill the days with things to say to you — while the nights try to haunt and tease me.... I look at those stars so far above, wondering if you're looking up even as I am — wondering if the stars are as bright for you in your place as I find them in mine.... But their brightness is cold, Annabel — lifeless. And again, the iciness descends and it's numbness I cherish.

"Then spring unfolds. The green scent of tilled earth rises. The waters thaw and rains come, calling forth the fresh buds. And the ache slowly awakens again as the ices melt — slowly, subtly like a leaf unfolding about a hidden apple blossom the pain returns. Yet so sweet too, like the first honey of the season — sparkling, like the late frosts which nip and bite. But I can't run from the hurting then. How can I? It means summer is beckoning... and summer means you."

I turned a bleak, haunted stare to her then, finding Annabel is standing so still as she watches me. Fear bit deep and sudden... she had to understand. She had to — or I would lose her.

"And now you ask me, where is the life that is my own?" My voice turned hoarse with scalding tears. "A life that is spent in such waiting? In such an empty hollow shell?

"Isn't it the summer I call my own, Annabel? Because you're here to share and tease and love and battle? Because this is the only season I find myself whole and sane?" The fear grew suffocating. I couldn't tell if — didn't she understand?! "Are you truly going to send me away without you? How could — could you do that?" I found myself shaking my head as she started towards me, "Why would you do that to me? To us? Why—?"

Her arms closed about me as I stifled a sob and I gripped her fiercely, pleading, "Don't do this to us! Please don't?!"

"No, shh — Jenny, I'm here," she hushed me, taking my face between her hands and wiping my tears away with her thumbs. "I'm here, Wren. I'll not send you away, I promise... I promise." Her lips were salty against mine and as warm as the warmth of a midsummer's afternoon.

She laughed then, breaking us apart and nodding behind me towards the hallway beyond the screen door. "The servants will be gossiping for weeks if we stand here — come on."

I followed her to the table, as I swiped at my wet cheeks with back-handed awkwardness.

"Here—" her smile was gentle as she presented me a clean kerchief. "Poor Wren, you never have learned to cry gracefully, have you?"

I blew my nose and shrugged, drying my face. "I can still learn—"

"No." Her fingers brushed the hair from my forehead, and those cinnamon-hued eyes devoured me with a most loving gaze, "I prefer you just as you are, I think... sniffles and all."

"You'll come?" I asked again, lost in the depths of her eyes.

"If you want me to."

"I do."

"Then I'll come."

But my own fears of manipulation had been raised now. And I hesitated, desperately afraid to ask for what I needed to hear.

Her fingers reached up again to softly smooth the furrows from my brow. "What is it, Wren?"

"Do you want to be with me, Annabel? Or is it just a way to escape Edward?" I couldn't believe it had sounded like that! I tried to shake the words away, but her fingers fell to my lips and held me silent.

"Listen to me carefully, Jenny-wren," Annabel stared at me levelly, her voice strong with her honesty. "You — our love — has been the only sane thing in my life since this whole muddled, disastrous mess with Dickie began last fall. The only thing that has kept me going was the impossible hope that some way — somehow, I would find a way back to you no matter what happened to Grandmama. I love you. I love you as a friend. I love you as my lover. And most importantly, I love that you love me. Through all of this winter, nothing has changed that. I have no intention of ever letting anything change that... as for the rest, you have to answer it for yourself."

"I love you," I murmured readily. "And I have no plans to change that either. I swear."

"Then—" she sighed, weariness overtaking her again, and I remembered how badly she'd been sleeping before last night, "I think we have some planning to do."

I picked up the tea pot as she sank into a wicker chair with a weak smile.

"What?" I prompted, passing her a cup.

"I'll never get used to someone in blue jeans pouring."

"I dare say you will," I chuckled and took my seat, "in twenty or thirty years."

Her expression softened, losing a hint of her fatigue. It was a thought that pleased her.

Chapter Twenty-one

I shoved my hands into the pockets of my denim jacket to keep from fidgeting. The mist was thick again, with the morning sun barely visible as a pale disk on the horizon. But it was just as well, I thought. This was the sort of weather accidents happened in, and it was comforting to know my lake was colluding with us instead of against.

The murmur of voices came from the kitchen. I heard Annabel pause, door half ajar as Mrs. Hodges said something about passing on her farewells to me.

I dropped to a squat in case the housekeeper approached the door. It would be better if Mrs. Hodges just didn't see me — let alone the two satchels and the portfolio of Annabel's which lay at my feet.

The door closed and Annabel's form appeared out of the fog, her teeth already chattering some. I held out my sheepskin coat for her. With a shiver, she discarded the shawl and shrugged into the coat gratefully.

I hugged her, turning up the collar to cover her ears. "Ready?"

She looked rather small, bundled up like that and her eyes were quite round as she nodded.

"You all right?"

"No!" Annabel rasped suddenly, heatedly. "I'm frightened witless. I just lied to a dear and trusted old friend who in about an hour is going to start dreading for my safety and in about two hours is going to think I'm dead. I'm worried about Grandmama. I'm furious at Dickie for creating this whole fiasco, and I'm too blasted cold to stand here arguing about how I feel! So for crying out loud — get me out of here before I change my mind!"

And with that she grabbed a bag and her portfolio and headed for the beach.

"Grandmama was awake?" I ventured quietly as I caught up with her.

"Yes...," and I knew I had found the real cause of her mounting fears. The others we had talked through, but Grandmama — she was a loyalty hard to discard.

"How was she?"

"Wretched," Annabel mumbled. We marched past the trees, ducking beneath the dripping leaves as we went. "She's not sleeping again — anticipation of Dickie's arrival I think. That may be the only good thing to come of this charade."

"What?"

"If he's so busy looking for my waterlogged body, perhaps he'll leave her alone."

I suppressed a grim sigh.

"I hope they're not going to miss these," but she was only fretting now, not really worrying about the cases in hand. "With all the hustle'n'bustle of packing in Philadelphia, I'm sure the luggage wasn't counted properly. I know at least half-a-dozen pieces were added and discarded at the last minute."

"If Mrs. Hodges puts this together, she'll only be relieved, Love. She's not about to say anything to your brother."

A mirthless laugh responded to that. "As if he'd have any chance of reaching us, even if he get lucky enough to guess where to look."

I refrained from comment. In another hour or so, Grandmama and M'dam Randolph would be setting their "magics" aside. At that point, neither Annabel, I nor even Mr. Thomas would be able to return to

Grandmama's era... and Dickie certainly wouldn't be capable of slipping forward into the 1980's. I put down Annabel's case and my knapsack next to the canoe. "Give me your shawl, Love."

She did and mutely I trudged off along the beach path. Some fifty feet along the walk, there was an abandoned yacht house with a break wall on its beach front. The lake's rock shelf disappeared there, bringing deeper water all the way into the stone wall. It was a scenic place to sit and watch a sunset — but if one fell in, there was no place to climb out for a good twenty-five feet to either side. And the current might do anything with its odd undertow in that mix of depths and shallows... especially to someone who didn't know how to swim.

I found a crack in the mortared stones of the break wall and wedged a corner of Annabel's shawl in tightly. There was no breeze so early in the day, but I made certain it would hold against a good wind. It would be there, even if it took Dickie a full day to find it. More than likely, however, it would be retrieved well before lunch today.

My stomach turned at the nasty implication of Annabel drowning. Given their parents' deaths, it was not going to be easy for Dickie to cope with... but it was the most practical and the most plausible pseudo-accident available. At this late date, we didn't have the time to get more creative.

Annabel was standing at the foot of the dock, gazing into the lake's mists, when I returned. I joined her, sliding an arm about her shoulders gently.

She glanced up at me after a moment, then buried her face in my shoulder as my grasp tightened.

"Ready?"

She nodded and turned.

The canoe grazed coarsely against a rock or two as I pushed off. I settled in and the paddle maneuvered us clear of the last scrape. So low set in the water, the mist seemed like the milky cloud layer it was... hovering a foot or two above the calm waters.

Annabel's faith in me was touching. Not once did she ask if I could see to guide us home. But then she had spent enough summers on this shore to know, this fog would lift before we even reached the middle of the lake.

"I'm glad she chose you, Jenny."

I looked at that huddle figure who was gazing so determinedly ahead.

"I'm glad she did too, Love."

The water lapped around us, friendly in its morning welcome. A heron called, its bright cheer reaching through the foggy veils.

I watched as Annabel's shoulders began to lower, slowly releasing the grief — the pain of the parting. Decisions had been made. All that could be done had been done. Love, time, and patience — things for both of us would come into place.

"I think," Annabel broke our silence gently, "I should finally learn how to swim, shouldn't I? And maybe... it's time to buy my own pair of blue jeans?"

"Maybe it is."

The silence lingered. The slight swish of my paddle blending well with both our quiet and the lake's lazy awaking.

"Still... maybe not." Annabel laughed suddenly. It was such a happy sound that she caught my breath. And then she stilled my heart as she amended, "No, not right now! I can't quite see myself clad in demins every day. Not yet. Can you, Wren?"

With rising spirits, I echoed her laughter,

"Well... certainly not every day."

But what a wonderful thought, not right now. It implied a later... a later that never again would hold a summer's end for Annabel and I.

What an incredibly, wonderful thought.